Isabelle
AND THE BEAST

MARIE SOLEIL

2

ONCE
UPON A
ROMCOM
BOOK 2

For Lola,
Thank you for all your help with every one of my books.
Oh, and thank you for introducing me to Seven Brides for Seven Brothers.
Nothing like Ben during the winter scene 😄

Contents

CHAPTER

One

ISABELLE

This is how I die: driving up a steep road with narrow twists and turns, set to the soundtrack of *The Sound of Music*. It's almost *too* ironic that the Mother Abbess is singing "Climb Every Mountain" as I slowly make my way up this ridiculous road.

"I hate my dad," I mutter to myself, gripping the steering wheel even more tightly. It's all *his* fault I'm endangering my life, driving up this winding mountain road to the giant mansion where Adam Stone, Hollywood movie star turned pariah, has been hiding for the last eight months.

I'm not nervous about meeting him just because he's a celebrity. I've been surrounded by famous people my whole life. My dad, who's a manager for a few big names in Hollywood, has brought his clients around our family home ever since I was a little girl. And my much-older sisters are supermodels, known around the world for their poise and beauty. So meeting a household-name actor shouldn't shake me up as much as it does.

But this is *Adam Stone*. Hollywood hothead. The former star who punched fellow actor Tristan Jackson last fall on the red carpet of the Goldie Awards and then...disappeared.

I'm going to suck it up and be brave, though. Because now, *I'm* one of my dad's clients. And I *finally* have the chance to score a leading role in a movie. Granted, it's a cheesy rom-com for one of those family-friendly channels, the Family Entertainment Network. But I've been trying to get a role besides "Barista #3" for years, and this is my chance.

And who do they want to star alongside me?

Adam Stone.

As terrified as I am of him and his reputation, having a huge name like his next to mine would do incredible things for my career. It hasn't been easy getting a role that fits my "quirks," as my dad likes to say. Most casting directors like to say I'm pretty enough (gotta love how superficial show business can be), but that my personality is a little too "whimsical" and "unconventional."

So finally, FINALLY, I fit the role, and it's actually to be the lead.

Now I just have to convince Adam Stone to do it with me. I'm sure the producers could find some lower-named actor to play my love interest, but they *really* want Adam. Something about making the Family Entertainment Network seem like a more legitimate production company.

But convincing him to do the role will be a task in and of itself. My dad, who is both Adam's manager and mine, asked him to take the role, and Adam said he'd consider it, under one condition:

That I come up to his secluded mansion and meet him myself.

Shouldn't be a huge deal, right? Except that Adam Stone has been hiding at this giant "castle" for almost a year, immediately after he punched a fellow actor *in the face* at the Goldie Awards.

No one has seen or heard from him since.

So...yeah. I'm a little nervous. And this winding road on the edge of a mountain isn't doing anything to allay my fears. But it's just a quick meeting, and my dad reassured me that there was nothing to be afraid of, so here I am, being brave and handling the situation like a big girl.

The temperature has been dropping steadily as I've driven higher and higher. When I left my apartment in LA this morning, hugging my best friend and roommate Jen goodbye, it was a typical May morning—somewhere in the mid-sixties. A few hours later, I arrived at the bottom of this ridiculous mountain, on the outskirts of Brookhaven, California, and it was seventy-five degrees. Now, at three in the afternoon? It's forty-eight degrees.

"It's the middle of May," I say to no one but myself. Although I swear sometimes my car, Philippe, can hear me.

My GPS connection disappeared about twenty minutes ago, but according to the original estimates, I should be there in about ten more minutes.

As I'm contemplating my life decisions, I see white flakes falling from the sky.

"Is that...snow?" I gasp. In answer, Philippe decides to skid on the road. Not a huge amount, but enough that I grip the steering wheel a little tighter and slow down more than I already was. Philippe is *not* built for snow. He's just a Honda Civic with street tires. As long as I make it to the top of the mountain in the next few minutes, I think I'll be all right.

I try not to blink, keeping my eyes open every second so I don't accidentally make a wrong turn. The snow keeps coming down, thicker and thicker, and I'm starting to panic. *It's early May.* How on earth is there a snowstorm in Southern California in May?! I know Big Bear gets snow in the winter, but this far into spring seems pretty far-fetched.

My breathing is shallow, and I feel like I might start crying when I turn and see a giant stone building just ahead through the trees. I exhale, blowing through my lips, and now I almost start crying out of relief. I made it. I didn't die.

A forest surrounds the castle, and trees line the path on either side of my car. The enormous building looks like it's straight out of a Jane Austen novel, made from gray stone with turrets and towers. There's even stained glass on some of the side windows.

Slowly, I drive closer and into the circular driveway surrounding a fountain that must be in use when it isn't snowing. Which should be now. Because, after all, *it's May.*

A lithe man wearing a long peacoat and gray scarf stands at the front entrance, so I pull the car up to him and turn it off. He gingerly steps around my car to open the door for me, letting the freezing air rush into my car, causing goosebumps to rise on my bare arms.

"Hello, Ms. Lovett," he says. "Thank you for visiting us here at Stone Castle."

"Thank you for having me," I reply. I quickly slip on my heels—they were too tricky to wear while driving, so I made the trip barefoot. He offers me his hand, and I take it, carefully stepping out of the car and into the snow piled about an inch high. "Is it supposed to be snowing?"

He lifts his mouth in a half-grin. "They say the weather at the castle reflects the disposition of its resident."

My eyes widen. *Say what?!*

"But that's just a myth," he continues. "We occasionally get snowstorms in May. It's just the altitude."

"Oh." It still seems very unusual, but I'll take his word for it. I shiver lightly, not expecting the snow and therefore not wearing anything snow-appropriate. My deep purple tank top with black slacks and stilettos is not the right getup for this climate.

"Let's get you inside," he says. "I'm Lionel, Mr. Stone's butler. I take care of the goings-on in the castle. If you need anything while you're here, I'll be at your service."

"I won't be here more than a few hours," I say. "But thank you for your offer."

He presses his lips together in a small smile. "As you say." He guides me up the giant stone steps to the front door. "Careful, these can get slippery."

I guess wearing stilettos was an extra bad idea today. I'm cautious about taking deliberate steps to avoid any major injuries. When we reach the front double doors, Lionel lets go of me and opens the one on the right. "Please come in. I'll show you to the study. We have a fire waiting for you."

"We?" I repeat. "You and Mr. Stone?"

"Oh, not just us. There are many other employees who live here. You'll see."

I nod, stepping into the castle and wiping my feet off on the giant Oriental rug marking the entrance. I take a moment to look around, trying to understand my surroundings. Unfortunately, a lot of the lights are out and it's nearly pitch-black in here.

"Why is it so dark?" I ask.

"Mr. Stone prefers the lighting to remain dim," he replies, shutting the door behind us and grabbing a candle from the wall.

Where the heck am I? I feel like I've stepped through a time portal into the fifteen-hundreds. How completely wild.

"This way," Lionel says, leading me to a room on the right. I catch a glimpse of a grand staircase, wide with ornate railings leading up to the second story. We step inside the room, and just like he said, there's a giant fire roaring in the fireplace. I scurry over as quickly as my heels will allow and stand as close as possible without burning myself, rubbing my hands together to get warm.

"I'll bring you a blanket. Would you like some slippers as well?" Lionel asks.

"Slippers?" I look down at my feet, debating if I want to feel warm and comfortable or if I want to maintain the professional appearance that I think will be more convincing to Adam. Slippers sound incredible, but I'm on a mission. I need to convince Adam to star in this movie with me, then get the heck out of here, and I'm sure having some fuzzy bunnies on my feet won't be a point in my favor.

"No, thank you," I finally say. Even *I* can hear the disappointment in my voice.

"Later, perhaps," Lionel says. "I'll go find Mr. Stone and be back shortly."

I nod. "Thank you."

He leaves, and I keep rubbing my hands in front of the fire, looking around the study for clues about Adam and his family. But it's too dark to see much beyond the faint outline of a few paintings on the walls and a bookcase, and a pair of wingback chairs behind me by the fireplace.

Adam started acting about four years ago, but his career took off as soon as he began. My best friend and roommate, Jen Park, and I have made a point of seeing every one of his movies because...well, let's be honest. He's ridiculously good looking. He's got a rugged, masculine energy that just makes you believe he'll carry you to safety while a building explodes behind him. And yes, that was a scene in one of his recent movies. So, while action flicks aren't typically my thing, they are when Adam Stone is starring in them.

But he's got a reputation—and not a good one. Demanding, self-centered, and grouchy have all been used to describe him on set. To my dismay, my dad confirmed that yes, he's kind of a jerk.

Still, I'm willing to look past it all for the sake of my own career. This is finally my chance to make it big, and I won't look a gift horse in the mouth.

Lionel returns with a blanket, which I accept gratefully and wrap around my shoulders, and then I'm alone again. I rehearse my introduction silently, a big smile on my face to disarm him from the start. *Hi, I'm Isabelle. It's really nice to meet you. Thank you for having me come to your family's estate; it's lovely here.* No, I won't mention that I almost died driving up the road. *I'm so honored that Fred Armstrong thought of having me act alongside you! I hope we'll—*

My rehearsal is cut short by the door banging open. I jump in surprise, dropping the blanket to the ground, then look over at the door and let out a yelp.

Because standing in the doorway...

Is a giant beast.

It takes a moment to register that the giant, hulking figure in the doorway is not, in fact, a beast, but is Adam Stone. Although I feel pretty justified in my assumption. He's at least six foot three, with a body that should be chopping wood somewhere in the Appalachians.

But aside from his physique, his hair has grown out past his shoulders, and he has a full, grizzly beard. It's hard to see beyond his outline in the dim lighting. Still, even in the shadows, I can tell this is not the same Adam Stone I saw in *Quantum Directive*, the movie he starred in last summer where he was a suave British spy in a sleek black suit, fighting against terrorists who were plotting to use AI to take over the world. No, this Adam Stone is ominous and almost more animal than man.

"Hello, Isabelle," he says, his deep voice rumbling through the room. His faint British accent is audible here, unlike how he hides it for most of his movies.

I open my mouth to respond, but all words have escaped my brain. Wasn't I preparing some kind of introduction? I can't remember. Because I'm completely consumed with the sight of Adam Stone—well, *present* Adam Stone.

My dad had warned me he looked different. That the last eight months had changed him, both physically and emotionally. But I don't think anything my dad could have said would have prepared me for what's in front of me right now.

I swear, he could eat me and I wouldn't be surprised.

He doesn't say anything, just studies me with an icy glare. *Snap out of it, Isabelle!* I finally come to my senses, remembering that he's assessing me and my ability to act with him. Well, if he wants an actress, I'll show him an actress.

You are a brave warrior, taking on a legendary beast.

It's a game I play sometimes, even in real life. I find it comes in handy, especially when I'm working at my day job–a waitress at The Cheesecake Factory.

Yes, the stereotypes are alive and well for an aspiring actress in Los Angeles.

Whenever I have a difficult customer, I find a role that fits the situation and embody it fully. Kid having a tantrum? Mary Poppins. Picky customer? Remy, the rat from *Ratatouille*. So right now, I'm going to embody a brave warrior. Brave Warrior Isabelle isn't intimidated by the beast in front of her. Brave Warrior Isabelle knows she can slay him.

I straighten and find my voice. "Thank you for having me here. And I'm really glad for the opportunity to meet you."

His eyes widen in surprise at my sudden shift. I notice one of his eyes looks slightly different from the other, but it's too dark for me to tell why.

He takes a few steps forward. Brave Warrior Isabelle falters, and I take a step back. I didn't realize I was right up against a wall, and I bump into a picture frame, knocking it down to the floor with a crash.

"Oh, goodness, I'm so sorry." I turn and kneel to pick it up, face flaming with embarrassment. Hopefully, he doesn't notice in the dark. Through the cracked glass, the image of a happy family makes me pause. There's a father who looks a lot like Adam, a beautiful mother, and four children—three boys and one little girl with the longest, most golden blonde hair I've ever seen. I peer closer at the picture and realize the oldest boy is Adam.

"Is this your family?" I ask. I look up from the picture and am startled to realize Adam is standing directly in front of me. From where I'm kneeling on the ground, he looks even more ominous, towering over me.

"Give me that," he snaps.

I straighten and hold the picture out with my right hand, but he doesn't grab it right away. In fact, his hand kind of flails around, searching for it before he gets a firm hold. I didn't think it was that dark in here... Is something wrong with his eyesight?

He pulls the picture out of my grasp and scowls down at me.

"I—I'm sorry," I stammer. I'm not sure if I'm apologizing for the picture or for asking about his family or for him not seeing the picture in my hand, but I feel like this meeting is going in completely the wrong direction.

He doesn't move, just stands and stares. At this close proximity, I can now see a scar down his left eye, starting at the middle of his forehead and ending on his cheek. That eye seems slightly glossed over. But his other eye is just as piercing blue as I remember from the movies. Oddly enough, these new impairments don't make him any less handsome. If anything, they give him a more wild but manly appearance, like a warrior coming home from battle.

He catches me staring and turns quickly, his back now to me. "Dinner will be served in a couple of hours. I'll meet you in the dining room."

"Wait, what?" I ask. "What am I supposed to do until then?"

Adam doesn't answer my question, just walks out of the room. Lionel reappears. "Miss Isabelle, I'll take you to the Lily room now."

"I...but... I'm not supposed to stay here."

Lionel looks sympathetic. "I understand your hesitation. Would you like to leave? I can inform Mr. Stone."

Would I? No. I need to stay and have this conversation with Adam. That terrifying drive would have been for nothing, and I cannot have that.

"No. I'll stay." I follow Lionel out of the room. He shows me to the grand staircase that I spotted when I first walked in, and I follow him up the stairs. We turn right and walk down a hallway lined with paintings and sconces lit by candles. The long shadows along the walls should scare me, but I remind myself again that I'm Brave Warrior Isabelle, and I will not be afraid.

As we walk down the hall, I spot a few people peeking at us through cracked doors.

"How many people are here?" I ask.

"Sixteen," Lionel replies. "Well, seventeen now that you're here."

"So, there are fifteen servants?"

"Employees, yes," he replies. "Three cooks, two footmen, four cleaning women, one hairdresser—although she hasn't had anything to do these past months, two sewists—"

"Sewists?" I interrupt. "Why do you need them?"

Lionel shrugs. "You never know when you'll need a new evening gown or tuxedo. Then Brigette, the housekeeper, and I am the butler."

"I see." But I don't, really. This feels very Victorian England to me, and while I enjoy watching *Pride and Prejudice* every now and then, I'm not familiar with the hierarchy at play.

I do some quick calculations in my head. "But wait. That's only fourteen. You said there are fifteen workers here."

Lionel looks at me over his shoulder, eyes bright. "You're a sharp one."

I shrug a shoulder, and the corner of his lips tug up in a smile. "The fifteenth person is Theodore."

"Who's—"

"Here we are," Lionel says brightly, opening a door to our right. "The Lily Room." He stands next to the door, holding it open for me to enter.

I step into the room, but it's still too dark to see anything.

"Is there a light I can turn on?" I ask. "Adam isn't here, so he won't mind, right?"

"Yes." Lionel reaches for a switch on the wall, and the room lights up from a chandelier hanging on the ceiling.

This room is every teenage girl's dream come true. The walls are painted a light lavender, and the bedspread has purple lilies all over it. There's a canopy over the gigantic bed, and all the furniture is painted white. A few floral paintings line the walls, a white vanity stands in the corner, and lavender curtains frame the giant windows. I turn in a circle, taking in my surroundings, my mouth wide open in awe. "This. Is. Amazing."

"Agreed." Lionel has a smile on his face, but his eyes are sad.

"Whose room is this?" I ask.

He tilts his head but doesn't answer my question. "Brigette will be here soon to get you ready for dinner." He bows his head and leaves the room.

Okay, first of all, why is everyone being so weird? And second, why does Brigette need to "get me ready" for dinner?

And third, what the heck am I supposed to do for the next few hours?

I sit on the bed, bouncing a few times for good measure. The mattress feels like a cloud. Too bad I'm not staying overnight.

But that's for the best, especially since I have a shift at The Cheesecake Factory tomorrow afternoon. Not that I'd really be disappointed to miss it. The other girls who work with me are... well, they remind me of the mean girls in high school. I've never really "fit in" with the crowd. Who wants to hang out with the weird girl who bursts into "Do Re Mi" from *The Sound of Music?*

Thankfully, Jen Park did. We met in high school. She was the tech-obsessed nerd, I was the theater nerd, and we bonded over being too weird for the cool kids. And after college, we found an apartment together in LA and have been pretty much inseparable.

I shoot her a text message, knowing she's waiting for all my updates on this adventure.

ME

I'm here in the castle. He's making me wait for dinner in this gorgeous bedroom, but I'm kind of creeped out.

JEN BFF

OMG what is he like? Is he just as handsome in real life as he is in the movies??

My fingers hover over the keyboard. How in the world do I explain the transformation of Adam Stone from sleek and suave British spy to mountain man?

A text comes in from my dad before I can respond to Jen.

DAD

Did you make it up safely?

ME

Yep. It started snowing though. Totally weird. I'm waiting in a bedroom for dinner.

DAD

It was pouring rain when I was there. Glad
you're safe. Let me know when you're on your
way home.

ME

A knock sounds on the door.

"Come in," I call, setting my phone on the bed next to me.

An older woman walks in, her brown hair with streaks of gray in a loose, low bun. She's short and looks like she'd give the best hugs, with lots of cushion. With a warm smile on her face, she says, "Welcome to Stone Castle, Miss Isabelle. It's nice to meet you. I'm Brigette."

Her smile is contagious, and I grin back at her. "Hi, Brigette. It's nice to meet you."

"I met your father when he was here before," she says cheerfully. "I can see the similarities."

"Can you? Most people say I look like my mother, but I don't remember her. I've only seen a few pictures."

Brigette's mouth parts. "Oh, dear," she murmurs. "I'm sorry for bringing it up."

I wave her off. "It's fine. She died when I was two, so I don't remember her."

To be honest, I wish I remembered her. Even more, I wish my dad and sisters would talk about her. I've only heard a few stories from my dad's friends who occasionally stop by to reminisce about the old times. But for some reason, my dad and sisters refuse to speak about her—ever.

"Can I help you get dressed for tonight?" Brigette asks brightly, drawing my attention back to her.

"Dressed?" I repeat, looking down at my clothes. "Why would I need to get dressed?"

"You don't need to, I suppose." She eyes my outfit suspiciously. "But there are many dresses to choose from here. I thought you might enjoy wearing something a little more..." She waves her fingers in the air and shimmies her shoulders.

I widen my eyes at her. "A little more what?"

"Fun!" She whisks into the room and opens the closet at the end of the room. It's not like the tiny rack of clothes I have in LA. This is a full-on *room* of clothes and shoes, with rows of racks.

"Whose clothes are these?" I ask, trying again to find out who this room belongs to.

"Miss Lily's," Brigette replies, her hands reverentially grazing the dresses. She looks back at me, her eyes narrow. "Although you're quite a bit taller than her. Any dresses you want to wear would need to be altered."

"I don't need to alter Lily's dresses." I'd also like to add, *Who the heck is Lily?* But I hold back because everyone seems so secretive.

Brigette waves a hand at me. "It's no problem. We have seamstresses available. They don't have much work to do, now that Mr. Stone..." She cuts herself off, turning back to the dresses. "Well, you know."

"No, I really don't."

She shrugs, still not facing me. "He tends to keep himself in more...casual wear these days."

"Ah." Honestly, I didn't look much at his clothes, since I was so taken aback by the hair, beard, and scar, but now that she mentions it, I think he was wearing a baggy sweatshirt and sweatpants. Which is extra unusual, considering his former reputation as a snazzy dresser, even when going to Starbucks or the grocery store.

I wave Brigette off. "I don't want to alter any of Lily's dresses, since I'm barely staying a few more hours. It's one dinner. I'm happy to stay in my current clothes."

"Suit yourself," she says with a shrug. "Shall we at least do your hair?"

"My hair?" I pull at the brown strands I've curled into waves. "No, thank you."

Brigette looks so disappointed that I want to give her something to do, but I also think this is all so WEIRD.

"Well, if you need anything, I'm just a ring away." She motions at the bell hanging next to the door. And not an electric bell. An actual metal bell.

I repeat, what century am I in?

"Thank you so much," I say, mustering up as much genuine gratitude as I can manage. They must not have a lot of visitors up here, and she must have been excited to have something to do. What can I have her do for me that doesn't involve getting me dressed or made up? "Maybe you can just tell me a little bit about the castle?"

"Oh, certainly!" She smooths her skirts and smiles widely. I sit back on the bed and she settles into the seat at the vanity to tell the tale.

"The Stone family moved from England to the United States nearly twenty years ago. At the time, it was just Mr. and Mrs. Stone with their three boys. Adam is the eldest, and he was twelve years old. Henry was ten, and Peter was seven."

I've heard about Adam's brother, Henry, who is next to inherit his father's company and recently got engaged, but I didn't know about the younger brother. Brigette makes it sound like there are more siblings, but I wait and listen patiently.

"They settled in Silver Lake City, where Mr. Stone founded Stone Technologies, but his wife dearly missed their estate in the English countryside. So Mr. Stone had this home built, here in the hills of Brookhaven, and they would come here for an escape whenever possible. Mrs. Stone would come frequently with the four children, even if Mr. Stone was busy with business."

"Four children?" I repeat.

"Ah, yes. Lily was born one year after the family moved here." Brigette's eyes light with the memory of her.

Aha. This is her room. And that explains the family picture I knocked over.

"The boys were so enamored with her. She was like their little doll."

The image of the family is slowly coming together in my mind. But why was Adam so secretive when I asked about the picture?

"She won't mind if I'm using her room?" I ask.

"No, of course not," Brigette dismisses me quickly. "She hasn't been here since...well..." She stands abruptly, her face pale. She shakes her head. "I've said too much. Let me know if you need any assistance in preparing for dinner."

She curtsies quickly and scurries out of the room, making me wonder what secrets are hiding in the walls of this castle.

CHAPTER
Three

ADAM

I slam the door shut to my office, inhaling and exhaling to calm my nerves.

Isabelle is NOT what I expected.

I *did* expect a measure of beauty. Her older sisters, Catherine and Joanna, are famous models and are very well known in the entertainment industry for their incredible beauty. Granted, most anyone can look beautiful when they have a professional team of hairdressers and makeup artists.

Isabelle, however, is striking.

She doesn't have the look of a model, but I prefer that. If anything, she has a "girl next door" look, if the "girl next door" is the stunning angel every boy in the neighborhood has a crush on. She's beautiful without trying, something I haven't seen much in the last few years. Aside from my sister, Lily, of course.

So, yes. I expected Isabelle to be beautiful like her sisters, but not to this degree. Beyond physical appearance, I expected Isabelle to have the personality of her sisters. When I've run into them in person, the words to describe them are *vapid* and *shallow*.

On the other hand, Isabelle is...perceptive.

Originally, I was just going to have her sit for a few minutes while I grilled her on her acting experience and made sure she wouldn't ask any personal questions or get too afraid. Now I'm the one who's backpedaling.

But I could see the wheels in her brain turning as she watched me, discovered my scar, and even analyzed the photo from my childhood. The one I currently hold in my hands. She noticed the difficulty with which I tried to take the picture from her grasp. She must know something is off with my eyesight, but I'm unsure if she can tell that I'm completely blind in my left eye. The doctor says my sight may return, but I know the truth. It's gone.

With all those things combined, I changed the plans and told her to stay for dinner.

I look down at the photo in my hands, one I hadn't paid attention to in years. It's a picture from about fifteen years ago, a memory of better times. A pang shoots through my chest. Sometimes I wish I could just go back.

I stride over to my desk and set the frame down by my computer monitor. I'll have to put it back in the study later. The sticky note on my desk reminds me why I'm going through all of this trouble. My list of sponsors, almost completely deleted, is down to two companies—LuxeLife Apparel and VerveTech. Everyone else has dropped me, and I can't necessarily blame them.

My phone buzzes with a text from Jim Lovett. A.k.a. my manager. A.k.a. Isabelle's dad.

JIM LOVETT

Hope things are going well with Isabelle. Please call me tonight after you're done speaking with her. We have an issue with LuxeLife.

There goes another sponsor.

I'm getting desperate.

I wish I weren't in this position. And I have no one to blame but myself.

And Tristan.

When I got my first starring role, Tristan Jackson, Hollywood's Golden Boy, reached out to me. As a former child actor who grew up in the business, he offered to give me some advice —including financial advice. I was stupid and naive, and I trusted his suggestion to invest in a start-up his friend, James Hook, created.

But when the start-up crashed and burned, so did my savings. And Tristan just laughed in my face.

I cut Tristan from my life and earned the reputation as the Hollywood Hothead, while he continued rising as everyone's favorite romance actor. Is it my fault I wanted my costumes to fit a certain way, and that my coffee had to be piping hot first thing in the morning? I think not. I'd been able to mostly avoid him until he sidled up to me at the Goldies eight months ago, describing his plans with my little sister, Lily, while smiling for the cameras and...

Well, that's enough of that. My hands are tightening around my phone just thinking about the memory, and I don't need my anger with Tristan to cause me to do something completely rash. Despite the temptation to hurl my phone against the wall, I hold back. Besides, I just did that a couple of weeks ago. Lionel doesn't need to make the trip down the mountain to get me a new phone again. But I let the anger fuel my drive to work harder, to protect my sister and keep the promises I've made her.

My financial situation wasn't a huge problem when I had movie deals coming in to replace that lost income. But now that I've become a complete outcast, I'm running out of options. And crawling back home to my father and brother like a dog with its tail between its legs isn't an option. I abandoned everyone after my mother died, and I'm sure my father wants nothing to do with me.

So, yes. I need to make this movie work. Even though it's a *GAG* rom-com. I've never filmed anything light-hearted and "fun." To me, a truly fun movie involves a lot of explosions and action. Some kissing is fine, as long as it isn't the focal point.

But a movie that centers on love and romance?

Count me out.

Except I don't really have a choice. No one wants me anymore. I already had a reputation of being difficult to work with. It's unlikely I'll be wanted by anyone else in the future, unless I make some kind of public apology, begging for Tristan's forgiveness and claiming I wish I could go back in time and change my actions.

The problem is I would absolutely, one hundred percent punch Tristan Jackson again if I had the chance.

But that's not understood by the public. And it won't be public knowledge, not when Lily is at stake.

What a mess.

I stand, about to get some kind of liquor to dull the ache in my mind, when I remember my promise to Lily. *No sad drinking, Adam.* I sink back into my seat, hearing her scold me for the stupid decision that originally led to my loss of sight in my left eye. For her sake, I'll handle this all while sober.

A knock sounds on my door. "Mr. Stone?" Lionel peers into the office, the only employee here allowed in this room.

"Yes, Lionel?"

"Ms. Lovett is in the Lily room. All is in order for dinner." He hesitates a moment.

"What is it?" I snap.

"Perhaps you would like to...change into something more..." His voice trails off, and he gestures at my clothes with his hand.

"No." My voice comes out like a bark.

"Sir." Lionel steps into the study with light, graceful steps. I've known him ever since we moved to the States when I was twelve years old and angry at leaving my home. He's seen me at my worst and my...

Well, no. He's really only seen me at my worst.

For some reason, he doesn't despise me. If anything, every time I snap at him, he tries to draw closer. If that's not some twisted logic, I don't know what is.

Lionel approaches my desk. "Might I remind you that your acquisition of this role depends, not only on your approval, but that of Ms. Lovett as well?"

Heaving a sigh, I run my hand down my beard. He's not wrong. Isabelle could decline the role. But I'm the more sought-after actor between the two of us. She's easily replaceable.

"She won't decline," I reply. "She's too eager to break into acting."

"I'm sure making yourself slightly more presentable wouldn't hurt, though."

"No, it probably wouldn't." Is Lionel right? Should I make sure she agrees to the part by changing into something less... homeless?

But here's the problem: if I change my clothes for her, that defeats the entire purpose of this meeting. I don't *want* a costar who's trying to change me, making me act a certain way or dressing how I don't want, or worst of all, speaking to her when I don't feel like it. Conversation and small talk are not part of the deal. I want to show up to work, do my job, go home, and get paid.

"I'm staying in these clothes," I decide. "And that's final."

Lionel shrugs and raises a brow. "As you wish, sir. Shall I prepare the dining room?"

I pause. "Let's wait another hour. This evening is on my timeline."

Lionel shakes his head in disapproval but doesn't say anything to argue with me. "I'll let you know when everything is ready."

He bows his head and exits the room, and I'm left wondering what Isabelle is doing while she waits.

Was this a bad idea? Am I setting myself up for failure?

No. If I'm getting back into acting, I want it on *my* terms. And if that means she needs to endure some discomfort, so be it.

CHAPTER

Four

ISABELLE

Two hours after Brigette left, Adam and I finally sit down for dinner.

At a gigantic dinner table that fits eighteen people.

Thankfully, we're sitting at one end together, not on opposite ends. But still—weird.

The room is dimly lit, just like the study, and my eyes are struggling to adjust. High-back wooden chairs with floral upholstery are placed around the table, and sconces with candles light the walls. A chandelier glimmers above us, but it must be on a dimmer because it's barely providing enough light to see our food.

Now that we're sitting here, I'm especially glad I didn't change into a fancy dress or do anything to my hair because Adam still looks like a mountain man wearing his sweatshirt and sweatpants. How ridiculous would I have looked in an evening gown when he's wearing sweats?

He hasn't said a word to me. He came in, sat down while eyeing me carefully, and is now eating his salad without acknowledging my presence.

I feel like screaming 'What do you want from me?', because

SERIOUSLY, why am I here? Why couldn't this meeting have been done over the phone, or even on Zoom? Couldn't he have gotten the information he needs from me in a *normal* manner? But no. I had to drive all the way up to this creepy castle and sit here with him...in silence.

I've got to figure this out. Guess it's up to me to strike up the conversation, even though HE'S the one with this grand idea of having me come up here to meet him.

I clear my throat. "The Lily room is beautiful. Your sister must love it here."

The instant scowl on his face tells me that was the wrong thing to say.

"How do you know about my sister?" he growls.

"I...I don't know anything about her," I stammer. I'm about to say that Brigette told me about her, but I worry that will get her in trouble, and she's too sweet to face Adam's wrath. So I stay quiet.

Adam grunts and stabs another forkful of salad.

"I loved *Second Chance Invasion*," I say.

He snorts a laugh. "Sure you did."

"Why do you doubt it?"

He finally looks over at me. "You saw *Second Chance Invasion*."

I nod. "Yes."

He sets down his fork and leans an elbow on the table. "What was my character's name?"

"Reginald. I thought it was a terrible choice, but you pulled it off."

His brows rise slightly in surprise, chewing thoughtfully. *Yes.* One point in my favor.

We finish our salads in silence while I rack my brain, trying to come up with topics of conversation that won't get me yelled at or ignored. Two young men—are they twins?—come out a minute later to take our salad plates and bring out the main course: chicken and pasta with a sundried tomato cream sauce.

"Thank you," I say to the man who leaves my plate. He smiles at me. Adam, on the other hand, completely ignores the man who served his dish.

"So, how did you get your first acting job?" I ask. "I know you didn't grow up acting. Did you study it in college? Or—"

"That's none of your concern." He doesn't even spare a glance in my direction.

"Oh." I pause. "I just thought it was cool you started acting later, you know, like me. I mean, I've always *wanted* to act, especially since my dad works in the industry, but I never got started until I was an adult."

He still says nothing, and I feel the urge to keep talking. At least, that's the only excuse I have for my word vomit. "My dad actually never wanted me to be part of it. My sisters were always so busy with their modeling jobs, beginning their careers as babies while my mom was alive. Instead of going that route with me, Dad tried to protect me as much as possible throughout my childhood. I guess I have to appreciate that about him. But I couldn't ignore the urge to act that was rolling under my skin, and once I finished college, I decided to go for it."

Adam sets down his fork and looks right at me. "Do you always talk this much?"

"I..." The truth is, sometimes. But I don't want to say that. He's making me so nervous, and I want to show him how friendly I am, that I'm trying desperately to fill the silence with proof that I'm a normal human being.

Unlike him.

So I try to be quiet for a few minutes. He's being exceptionally rude, but I want this role. And if he'd prefer I don't sit and chit-chat, I can try that for a little while.

"What else have you done?" he asks, breaking the silence.

I swallow the food in my mouth. "I'm sorry?"

"Acting. What other roles have you performed?"

I press my lips together. He's basically asking for my IMDb information, and I know my list doesn't sound great because I've hardly gotten any roles worth noting. Being an extra in an episode of *This is Us* is hardly worth mentioning. "I've been in a few shows and commercials."

"But no actual roles."

"Not yet, but—"

"You never got an actual role because you weren't good enough."

My mouth drops open at his bluntness. I'm at a loss for words. Did he really just say that to me?

And even worse, he continues speaking. "In fact, you probably never would have gotten this role if it weren't for your father pulling strings. Or did your sisters vouch for you this time? Either way, it's just a role for a made-for-tv rom-com on a ridiculous network, so it's not like it would have taken much effort in the first place."

My face flames with embarrassment and tears sting my eyes. How dare he speak to me like this! This is the final straw.

I slam my fork down on the table and stand, my chair loudly scratching the wood floor. Adam turns to face me, his eyes wide in surprise.

"You should be ashamed of yourself," I say sternly. "How dare you say those things! Who do you think you are that you can speak to people like that?"

Maybe that wasn't the smartest thing to say. He's Adam Stone, world-famous action star. Of course he can say whatever he wants. But I'm fired up now, and I'm not about to let anyone walk all over me.

If breaking into Hollywood means dealing with this jerk

every day, then I'm not doing it. My self-worth is too high to allow him to speak to me like this and walk all over me.

Adam's mouth drops. Has no one ever called him out? Probably not. Well, he needs a reality check, so he'd better buckle up, because I'm not done.

"You think you're better than everyone else, up here in your fancy family castle. But that doesn't make you a good person. And I refuse to spend another minute here, being disrespected like this." I throw my cloth napkin down on the table and turn to leave.

"Wait!" Adam calls, his voice slightly weakened. "So...the movie?"

I turn to face him, and for a moment, he actually seems worried. Good. Let this be a lesson for him. "There is no way I would *ever* be in a movie with you." I turn back to the dining room door and rush to the front entrance, which is thankfully just down the hallway and not through the twisting maze like the other parts of the castle. I make it to the front door, fling it open, and am nearly blown backward by freezing air.

I can't believe my eyes.

It's a full-on blizzard. White snow falls from the sky and has already covered at least three inches of the ground.

I'm still in shock. I step outside, feeling the cold seep into my high heels, but I don't care. Crunching through the snow, I spy Philippe. My beloved Honda Civic is covered in snow.

I can't move. I can't breathe. There's no way I can drive down the mountain now. Not with my street tires and snow covering the already perilous and winding road.

I have no other choice.

I'm trapped here.

CHAPTER

Five

ADAM

She said she won't do the movie.

Of all the scenarios I envisioned, this was not one of them.

Looking down at the food in front of me, my head spins. What am I going to do now? Do I run after her? Try to convince her to stay, passionately claiming I'm not really as terrible as I seem?

But would that be the truth?

Probably not.

There's nothing to prove. I'm just as much the monster she thinks I am. And I proved it by staying here in the dining room.

But a minute later, she reappears. Her eyes are wide, and there are white snowflakes in her hair.

"It's snowing," she says, her voice low.

And now I realize I'm back in the power position. I have the advantage. And I'm going to use it to the fullest.

I wait a moment. "Is it?" I reply.

She nods slowly. "And my car can't handle the conditions."

"Ah." I stab a piece of broccoli and take a bite, biding my time.

She presses her lips together. I know what she needs. She needs to stay here for the night, and it's killing her to have to ask. But I'm not going to make this easy for her, not when she said she didn't want to do the movie with me.

That wasn't supposed to be her decision. It was *mine*. And now she's ruined everything.

She finally clears her throat. "Since I'm unable to drive, do you think that I...would it be all right if I just..." Her voice trails off, and she gestures with her hand to fill in the blanks.

I stare at her blankly. "I'm sorry. What's the problem exactly?"

She crosses her arms across her chest and presses her lips into a firm line. "Can I stay here tonight?"

I set down my fork, folding my hands on the table. "Well, well, well, that's a little soon, don't you think?"

She probably can't see my smirk from across the room, but her mouth drops wide open. "I did *not* mean like that!"

"I don't know. You're the one asking to stay the night. In my experience, that only means one thing."

She gives a little yelp of frustration. I may have pushed too far.

Before I can salvage the conversation, though, she collects herself, straightening to her full height and slowly walking up to me at the table. She stands next to my chair and looks down at me, but I pick up my fork, keeping my eyes on my plate, and take a bite of chicken.

"Let me make myself abundantly clear," she says, her voice low and dangerous.

And sexy.

Crap.

"There is no universe in which I would *ever* ask to stay the night with you in...that way. We've spent barely thirty minutes together, and that has already become blatantly obvious. I am asking for you to find a shred of humanity, which I hope exists under this grizzly exterior, to allow me to stay overnight so I don't die in a blizzard."

I wish her words didn't sting. I wish they didn't cut me to the core and make me question our entire interaction today. A 'shred of humanity?' Does she really think I'm incapable of that?

I clear my throat. "Lionel. Make sure Brigette gets the Lily room ready for Ms. Lovett to stay overnight."

Lionel inclines his head and leaves the room.

"Thank you," Isabelle says. She turns and follows Lionel, and I notice her nearly untouched dinner plate. A pang of guilt runs through me. Not only did I make her wait for hours alone to eat, but now she won't even finish her dinner.

"Wait!" I call out before she's able to exit the dining room completely. "What about your dinner?"

Her eyes soften for a moment. Maybe she sees a 'shred of humanity' in me, after all. But her eyes narrow a second later. "I lost my appetite."

And with that, she leaves.

CHAPTER

Six

ISABELLE

"Adam Stone is the most insufferable man I have ever met in my life!" I flop face-first onto the bed.

Brigette chuckles, busily setting out towels and amenities for me. "He's not so bad."

I twist around, sitting straight on the bed. "Are you kidding me? I know he's your boss, so you probably have to say nice things about him, but COME. ON."

Brigette stops her scurrying and faces me, a stack of towels in her arms. "He can be a bit...gruff. I agree. But he's been through so much, especially after the accident. You have to understand..." Her voice trails off as her eyes widen, and she resumes her tasks in the room.

Accident? "Understand what?"

Brigette waves her hand at me. "It's nothing. Forget I said anything."

"I wish I could," I mutter. I rub my forehead, lamenting my fate for the evening. "I'm already freaked out about staying here. Are you sure he's not going to eat me in the middle of the night? I swear, he looks like a lion now."

Brigette snorts. "You'll be fine, as long as you stay out of his private office."

My mouth drops open. Would he really do something to physically harm me?

Brigette's eyes widen. "Oh, no! I didn't mean it that way! Well, you still shouldn't go in the office. But he would never do anything to harm you. That I can promise."

"What's in the office?"

"Nothing, nothing." Brigette keeps up her work, but I don't miss her hard swallow.

Well, now I'm paranoid. I don't ask any more questions, though, because Brigette is visibly flustered. She's been so kind to me, and I don't want to make her more upset than she already is. My stomach, though, has other ideas. It growls louder than the helicopter propellers in Adam's latest movie.

"Oh, dear. Are you hungry?" Brigette asks.

Yes, I'm starving, but I couldn't stomach another minute of sitting at the table with your boss. "No, no, I'm fine."

"You're not." She spins in a slow circle, triple checking that everything in the room is in order, then gives me a quick nod. "Come with me to the kitchen. We'll find you something to eat. And I can introduce you to the rest of the staff."

"Are you sure?" My stomach grumbles again, even louder this time.

Brigette smirks. "Positive. Come now, let's go." She steps into the hallway, and I follow her. "I can show you around the castle as well."

"I guess that's a good idea." Why not take advantage of the opportunity to explore this place? But fear pops in my mind. "Will Adam mind?"

"Hmm?" She turns to face me. "No, he should be in his office by now. He tends to spend his evenings in his quarters, which are on the other side of this upper level, so we won't have to worry about running into him."

With that weight off my shoulders, my stomach gives a grumble of approval. I follow Brigette through the maze of corridors, all dimly lit by candles. These are all bedrooms, but I could easily get lost in this place.

She points out Adam's quarters. "This is Mr. Stone's office, and next door is his bedroom. Everything here in the castle is available to you, just not Mr. Stone's quarters."

The little shiver of nerves reappears. Didn't Lionel say there was someone named Theodore here? Who is that, a dead body in the office? At this point, I wouldn't be surprised by anything.

"Why do I need to stay out?" I make my tone light, hoping she won't see through me to my racing heart. "Is he hiding a… body in there?"

"A *body*? No, no, of course not."

I want to be relieved, but her quick response still hasn't convinced me.

I need to get out of here ASAP.

I follow her down the stairs and she points out the different rooms as we pass them—the music room, the great hall, and the library. "And here's the kitchen!" she says brightly, pushing a swinging door open. The kitchen feels homey; the cabinets are all dark wood and the countertops are beautiful granite, gray mixed with shades of tan and brown. We're met with cheerful voices from a small group crowded around a long wooden table, talking, laughing, and relaxing after the day.

But as we enter the kitchen, I see the moment one of the young women about my age spots me. She elbows the girl next to her, and quickly the voices drop to whispers.

"This is Ms. Lovett," Brigette announces to the group.

"It's just Isabelle," I say, giving a small wave.

"I brought her here to get something to eat," Brigette explains.

There's a scuffle as the workers start getting out of their chairs and head to the kitchen. A man with a mustache smooths out his white chef's coat, and the two men who served dinner, the ones who look nearly identical, stand and straighten their lapels.

"No, please," I say quickly. "I just need a little snack. Maybe some cereal?"

The girls around my age, one redhead and one blonde, glance at each other with their eyebrows raised.

"Just cereal? Are you sure?" Brigette asks me.

"Yes, that would be great. It's my favorite snack at home. I used to stay up late watching Seinfeld with my dad and eating bowls of cereal."

Brigette smiles softly and leads me over to a pantry. She opens the door, and I'm met with a floor-to-ceiling stash of every cereal you can imagine. Cap'n Crunch, Lucky Charms, Trix (which, I can confirm, is NOT just for kids), Cheerios, and some healthy organic ones, too.

"Whoa," I breathe. "This place is like a grocery store." I turn to Brigette. "Do you have every kind of ice cream, too?"

"Sadly, no." She lifts the side of her mouth in a grin. "Mr. Stone's preferred late-night snack is cereal, as well."

"Hmph." That takes the wind out of my sails. A pit forms in my stomach remembering our conversation and the fact that I refused to do the movie with him. That movie was supposed to signal the start of my career. Now it's over before it even began.

I can't worry about that now. I look back at all the cereal options and smile again, grabbing the box of Cookie Crisp. "I was never allowed to eat this one at home. My sisters said it had too much sugar. But I've always wanted to try it."

"Sounds perfect." Brigette motions towards the girls, and

they set a bowl, spoon, and carton of milk on the table. "Come, eat."

I bring my prized box to the table and pour my cereal. "So, you all live here with Adam?" I ask. I take my first bite of the cereal and let out a little sigh. "Oh, this is good."

Brigette smiles. "Yes, we do."

"It's pretty secluded out here. Don't you guys have families?"

"We are each other's family," she replies. "But when the Stone family isn't here, we go back to our homes and families to visit."

"Huh. Interesting." I take another bite of my cereal, loving the fact that I finally get to enjoy this naughty treat. I guess I could have bought a box back home in LA, but there's something more fun about eating it here.

Now I notice everyone is staring at me.

"What are your names?" I ask. I might as well make some friends if I'm stuck here.

"This is Mario," Brigette says, motioning toward the man with the curly mustache and white ensemble. Stereotypes are alive and well here. "He's our head cook. Sophie and Maisie are his assistants." The two young women nod at me. "Graham and Greyson are our footmen," she says, and the two identical men in their twenties smile at me.

Brigette points upward. "Everyone else has gone to bed. Nina, Eva, and Becca are our cleaners, Cassandra is our hairdresser, and Josephine and London are our sewists."

There's no way I'm going to remember everyone's names from this single introduction, but at least I've got them stored somewhere in the back of my mind. It's kind of awkward that everyone is watching me. I'm about to tell them they can do something else, since their job does not include waiting on me hand and foot, but I'm interrupted by the pitter-patter of little feet rushing our way.

"Gramma!" A little boy with sandy blond hair rushes up to Brigette and squeezes her around the legs.

"Theodore! You're supposed to be in bed!"

He steps back and gestures at his green costume. "I'm not Theodore."

"Ah. I'm so sorry," she says with a smile. "Hulk, you're supposed to be in bed!"

In return, Theodore gives a little growl and flexes his muscles, then hugs Brigette's legs again.

Ohhh, so *this* is Theodore.

Not a dead body.

That's a relief.

But then it raises another question. "Why does your grandson live here?" I ask Brigette.

"It's just a visit," she says. "My son—his father—is on a much-needed vacation." She lowers her voice. "He's a single father now." She mouths the words *Theo's mom left.*

Poor little Theo.

She ruffles his hair. "So Theo gets to have some fun here with us. But it might turn into a longer stay than we expected, with this turn of the weather." She looks down at Theodore, who still has his arms wrapped around her legs. "Theo, this is Isabelle. She's staying here tonight."

He eyes me carefully. I'm not an expert on kids, but I'm pretty sure he's around preschool age. "Hi, Theo. It's nice to meet you."

"You're eating candy cereal," he replies. "Daddy doesn't let me eat that kind of cereal."

"Well, my daddy didn't let me eat this kind of cereal when I was a kid, either."

He considers this for a moment, then looks back up at Brigette. "Can I have some of that cereal, too?"

Brigette looks at me, and I shrug. I'm not in the position to make decisions like this, but I don't see why he can't have a treat with me.

"Sure," she says.

Theo squeals and expertly climbs up the counter, grabbing a bowl and then plopping down into the seat next to me. I pour some cereal and milk in his bowl, and with a cheeky grin aimed at me, he takes his first bite.

"Yummm," he says, diving in for another bite.

"Slowly, Theo," Brigette warns.

Theo growls back at her.

"Slowly, Hulk," she tries again. He gives her a big grin and nods.

"He's got quite an imagination, huh?" I whisper to Brigette.

"You have no idea." She smiles wistfully at him. "You never know which superhero he'll be that day."

"How does Adam feel about him being here?" I ask.

Brigette tilts her head from side to side. "He tolerates it, so long as Theo doesn't cause too much trouble. Which is usually Becca's job...Theo, where is Becca?"

Despite his mouth full of cereal, he answers. "She's asleep in my bed. She's veeeeery tired."

"I thought Becca was a cleaner?" I ask Brigette.

"When Theo visits, she doubles as nanny. But she tends to fall asleep early."

I snort a laugh. "I'm not surprised."

Brigette sighs. "Keeping an eye on a three-year-old can be very exhausting."

"I'm three and a half!" Theo gestures widely with his hands, and his spoon flings milk across the table.

I've finished my cereal, so I stand and take my bowl to the sink while one of the other girls cleans up Theo's mess. "I should text my dad and let him know I have to stay overnight. He wanted me to call when I was on my way down the mountain."

"Oh, you probably won't be able to do that." Brigette says.

I whip my head over to her. "What do you mean?"

"When the weather is this bad, we typically lose cell service. And general phone service."

My brain needs a second to process her words.

No cell service.

Or phone service at all.

"Wait, so we're STRANDED up here?!" My voice comes out like a squeak.

Brigette exchanges a nervous glance with the other workers. "I mean...in a way, yes. But I promise, you're safe. You don't need to worry."

My heart races in my chest. She seems genuinely kind, as do the rest of the workers. And if Theo is here, there shouldn't be anything to really worry about.

Right?

But that doesn't ease the voice in my head telling me I'm trapped...with Adam Stone.

CHAPTER

Seven

ADAM

I sabelle is staying here.

Tonight.

I'm not sure why this affects me so heavily. Her father stayed overnight a few months ago, when I first told him I needed Isabelle to come meet me here, and I didn't give him a second thought.

But knowing Isabelle is here turns my mind in circles. I can hear her in the kitchen with the workers. They might as well be putting a show on for her with how loud they're being. But it doesn't bother me, so long as she doesn't come here, into my office.

Fire from the fireplace lights the room as I peruse my paperwork. More letters from lawyers, one of whom is my cousin, Bethany Stone, down in Canyon Cove. We have so many issues that one lawyer wasn't enough.

Lionel walks into the office carrying a steaming cup of tea. "Here you are, Mr. Stone."

I nod as he sets it down on my desk, noting the moment he registers our family photograph's new home.

"Anything else you need this evening?" he asks.

I set my hands on the desk and look up at him. His face has grown long and thin with age. His hair, once a dark brown with some streaks of gray, is now completely white, and he wears his glasses at all times, not just while reading. This old man, though, knows me better than almost anyone else on this earth, and I trust him completely. He's the only one I can confide in.

"Has Isabelle settled in?" I ask.

He nods. "She's meeting the other workers in the kitchen, and her room is ready for her to sleep."

"Good. And...her clothing?"

"All set."

I pause, and Lionel notices. "Is that all?" he asks.

I glance at the frame on my desk. The cracks in the glass make it difficult to see my mother, a sensation I feel more and more lately. "Was I..." I clear my throat. "Did I go too far tonight?"

Lionel raises a brow at me. "Do I have permission to speak candidly?"

I nod, my long hair falling over my eyes. I brush it aside and prepare for what's sure to be a zinger from Lionel.

He takes a seat across from me. "Yes. I believe you did."

I knew he'd be honest. "In what way?"

He holds my gaze. "You not only insulted her ability, but you implied her unfair advantage because of her father's position."

I furrow my brow. "Was I incorrect?"

"As a matter of fact, yes. But that's beside the point." He leans his elbows on the desk. "Is it possible you're jealous of her relationship with her father, when you currently have little to no relationship with your own?"

Unfortunately, his comment struck a nerve. "Hitting hard, don't you think, Lionel?"

He sits back in his seat. "I apologize, sir."

He's right. I don't have much of a relationship with my father. The only siblings I really talk to are Henry and Lily, and that's because Henry bailed me out of jail and handled the initial situation with the lawyer.

I clench my jaw. "Even still, she didn't have to disagree so vehemently."

"No, she didn't." Lionel presses his lips in a smile. "But I'm glad she did."

"I don't understand. Now she won't do the movie with me."

Lionel eyes me cautiously.

"Go ahead, Lionel."

He heaves a sigh. "I don't believe anyone has chastised you so effectively since...well, since your mother passed."

Talk about a dagger to the heart.

Lionel continues, undeterred. "Your mother knew exactly how to keep you in line, even as an adult. And you loved and respected her so much that you truly listened to her. But over the last five years, ever since she passed, no one has had the courage to...well, set you straight." He pauses, assessing my expression. "I've said too much." He stands, pushing his chair back. "I apologize for overstepping."

"No. I asked for it." Even though that's the truth, I don't stop him when he bows as a farewell and exits the room. I'm not ready for more truths from him.

Is he correct? Was my mother truly the last person who would *call me out*?

After her death, nearly five years ago, I left everyone in our hometown of Silver Lake City and moved to Hollywood. My father was devastated. He had been training me to take over the family company, Stone Technology, the largest tech company in the world. But I didn't care. Besides, my younger brother Henry was always the better fit. I wanted to leave, far away from anyone and anything that reminded me of my mother. That included my father and my three younger siblings.

Although now I look back and know I should have stayed. Lily was only fourteen. My father was grieving. But at the same time, so was I.

By some miracle, I quickly got my first role in a movie. Unlike Isabelle, who has been playing parts as an extra for years, I got my first leading role less than six months after arriving in Hollywood. Perhaps it was this quick ascension to fame, combined with the failed investment with Tristan, that made me the "Hollywood Hothead." I was demanding on set, but no one told me otherwise. I was a star, and I could have whatever I wanted.

Look where it got me. Stuck in my castle with a scar and a malfunctioning eyeball.

For nearly my entire life, aside from my parents and siblings, all I've heard is, "Yes, Mr. Stone," and "What can I do for you, Mr. Stone?" I've soaked it all in.

But I didn't realize how much I missed the voice of someone putting me in my place until tonight.

Maybe Isabelle doesn't want anything to do with me, but I need to see more of her.

Eight

ISABELLE

I t's three a.m., and even though I'm snuggled under the covers in the most comfortable bed I've ever laid in, I haven't slept a wink. And it's not because I'm afraid.

Well, it's not ONLY because I'm afraid.

I've always struggled with falling asleep, ever since I was a little girl. My dad did his best to comfort me, but he was so busy working and isn't exactly what I'd call an emotional father. I especially feel this now, as he tries to juggle being both my father and manager. Most of the time, the manager side wins out. And my sisters...well, they considered me little more than a nuisance. So my dad's solution to my sleep problem was simple: I had a tiny TV in my bedroom with a DVD player attached, and I'd watch *The Sound of Music* or *Seven Brides for Seven Brothers* and fall asleep to the music and dancing.

This has turned into a daily ritual—nay, a necessity. Now that technology has advanced, I don't have to rely on carrying around DVD copies of my favorite movies. I can stream them all on my phone.

Except for when there's no Internet.

Boo-hoo, first world problems, right? I know, I'm ridiculously spoiled. But I haven't had a night without my movies in years. The last time I tried to sleep without them was at a slumber party my sophomore year of high school. I ended up calling my sister Catherine to pick me up early.

It was a killer for my social life. I was already the weird girl who was super into classic movies and musicals, and after this embarrassing episode, only Jen wanted to be my friend. But hey, it turned out to be research for my future career.

Although, who knows how much of a career I have to look forward to, now that I refused to do this role with Adam.

Oh, my blood boils just thinking about him tonight. His self-righteous attitude got under my skin in the worst way. I wish he didn't affect me so much, but I can't move past it. The implication that I'm only going to be successful because of my father drives me nuts. I've been working my butt off, acting in ridiculous, tiny roles for years, and never taking advantage of my father's reputation for a leg up.

And here was my opportunity. Finally. Sure, it wasn't going to be a huge Hollywood blockbuster, but it was still going to be a leading role in an actual movie. Now, because of stupid Adam Stone, I'm losing my chance.

I tell myself it's not the end of the world. There will be other movies. But producers talk, and if I say I won't do this movie because of Adam, maybe I'LL get labeled as "difficult to work with."

My career will be over even before it begins.

Ugh. If only I could just watch *The Sound of Music* and fall asleep to the captain singing "Edelweiss."

I've tried to lose my dependence on watching movies every night. A few years ago, I listened to a podcast about how important it is to get early morning and late evening sun for our bodies' rhythms. So, every morning, I drink my coffee out on the balcony of our tiny apartment in LA. And every evening, I take a walk around sunset time. My body's clock seems to have aligned better ever since I've done that.

But here...I'm trapped. And I keep hearing a voice in my head that says *outside, outside, outside.*

THE RICH SMELL of coffee is the only thing keeping me awake right now.

I THINK I fell asleep for a grand total of thirteen minutes last night, only because I kept imagining the "Favorite Things" scene from *The Sound of Music.* But Brigette came in around seven this morning, singing loudly and offering to do my hair and makeup. When she saw how tired I was, she offered to let me sleep in, but the damage was done. There was no more sleep to be had.

So now I'm here in the kitchen with the staff at eight, trying to wake myself up with coffee and sugar. I'm wearing silk purple pajamas that must belong to Lily, because the pants cut off at my calves. They're ridiculously comfortable, though, so even though they're super short, I'm willing to endure a silly appearance.

And Lionel made good on the offer for slippers. Somehow they had a pair of fuzzy pink bunny slippers in my exact size. I look like a child, but I'm too tired to care.

"Ms. Lovett?"

"Hmm?" The sound of Brigette saying my name snaps me out of my stupor.

"More coffee, dear?"

I sigh, leaning my forehead on the table and stretching my arm out. "Yes, please," I mumble.

Brigette chuckles as she fills my mug with more steamy goodness. "Rough night?"

"You could say that," I reply.

I don't know how I'm going to function.

And worse, I'm still stuck here. Because it's STILL snowing.

I'm trapped in this castle prison with hardly any light...and Adam Stone. I just pray I don't run into him anymore while I'm here.

"Are there any snow clothes I could wear? I'd really like to just step outside for a few minutes."

"In this storm?" Brigette shakes her head. "We do have snow clothes, but you'll have to wait until the snow lightens up."

My heart sinks. "What *can* I do today?" I ask. "Is there anywhere I can go to make sure I don't see Adam?"

"That desperate to avoid him?" she asks with a playful smile. She sets down the coffeepot and taps her lips with her finger. "You could head to the library. I think that would entertain you for some time."

I'm not much of a reader, but at this point, I'll do whatever I can to distract myself from the snow falling outside. If only I had cell service. At least I'd be able to watch something or even call Jen.

The cooks are working busily to prepare breakfast, and it smells amazing. Pancakes and bacon and eggs have always been my favorite.

"Do you make breakfast like this every day?" I ask Mario.

Mario nods and faces me. "Mr. Stone actually prefers oatmeal, but he allows us to make whatever breakfast we want for ourselves."

"Oh." That's actually pretty nice. I wouldn't have expected that from him.

A rush of footsteps alerts me to Theodore's presence. Today, he's wearing a skin-tight spandex Spider-Man costume. He stretches out his hand to me, keeping his middle and ring fingers pointed at his palm, and makes "CH-CH" sounds, like he's shooting a web.

"Well, good morning, Spider-Man," I say.

He crouches down on the ground, one leg straight out to the side. "I'm actually Spin."

"Ah, yes, of course." I don't know the difference, but apparently it matters to him. "Good morning, Spin. Are you ready to save the world today?"

He nods, his face solemn. "Green Goblin is in the library. I have to stop him."

"You can't go alone, Theo," Brigette pipes in. "Where is Becca?"

Theo shrugs.

Brigette sighs. "Isabelle, would you mind taking Theo to the library? It's just a few doors down from here, and Theo knows the way. Breakfast will be ready in about fifteen minutes. This way you can pass the time without falling asleep at the table."

I stretch my arms high above my head, trying to pump blood through my body. "Sounds good."

Theo holds his hand out to me, and with a smile, I grasp his tiny fingers. He pulls me with alarming strength out of the kitchen and into the main part of the castle.

"Do you like being here?" I ask. Even though Adam doesn't allow bright lights, the morning sun streams through the stained-glass windows, reflecting colorful lights all over the floor, and I can finally see the place more clearly. Red and purple velvet drapes hang from the windows. The walls are covered with paintings of the countryside; my guess is they're of their home in England.

"Yes. It's fun because there are a lot of places to hide."

I snort a laugh. "Where's your favorite place to hide?"

He eyes me suspiciously. "I can't tell you. Then it wouldn't be a hiding place anymore."

"Mm, true." I give him a serious nod. He seems appeased and keeps leading me through the halls.

I'm caught up studying the paintings and decorations in the castle, not to mention still half-asleep, so I don't immediately notice when the door to my right opens, and Adam Stone comes barreling out.

"Agh!" I cry. Not only am I caught off guard by his presence, but with the full sunlight on him, his appearance is even MORE shocking. How is this the man who portrayed Harry Ryland in *Live Another Day*, the dashing World War 2 hero who saved the United States from an alien invasion?

Yes, that was a real movie.

He seems just as startled to see me, almost like he forgot I was here, his eyes wide and piercing. Well, one eye. Now that the morning light is streaming in the castle, I can clearly see the scar over his left eye, from his forehead down to his cheek, and that eye is glassy. Still, I inhale sharply at the intensity of his full attention on me. For a moment, I can see the Adam Stone who made me swoon in the movies. It wasn't just about his grooming, but that intense gaze could make a girl fall in love.

But in a split second, his shock turns to disdain. Eyes narrowed, jaw set, he looks like the carnivorous beast from last night.

Brave Warrior Isabelle won't take his attitude. I look away and pull on Theo's hand. "Let's go."

I tip my chin up and walk past Adam, catching a glimpse of him watching me out of the corner of his eye. Maybe he's repulsed by the pajamas that are too short or the bunny slippers on my feet. Let him watch. I won't be afraid of him.

But a single word from him stops me dead in my tracks.

"Wait."

CHAPTER
Nine

ADAM

Why did I tell her to wait?

What exactly is she waiting for?

I'm not sure, but now that I see Isabelle in front of me, all I know is that I want to be near her. After speaking with Lionel, realizing how much she affects and challenges me, I haven't been able to stop thinking about this beautiful woman.

She's wearing Lily's pajamas, which are understandably short on her, and a pair of bunny slippers. My mother always loved wearing them and kept a full stash in all sizes for guests here at the castle. Isabelle's attire is slightly ridiculous but also endearing.

Her eyes are tired, though. I thought Lily's bed was comfortable, but perhaps she's nervous about being here. I'll have to ask Brigette to check on that later.

"Where...are you going?" I finally ask.

"To the library," Theodore says, still with his hand firmly in Isabelle's. "She's bored."

Isabelle shrugs. "No cell service, no Internet, so I need something to do while I'm here."

"Hmm." I'm not sure how to ask if I can come along without

seeming strange. After all, I was exceedingly rude to her last night. But I want to know more and learn more about her, the woman who dared to tell me off and refused to be in a movie with me. I should hate her, shouldn't I? Instead, I want to be with her even more.

"Do you want to come with us?" Theodore asks.

Bless him. "I suppose so," I say, feigning nonchalance. I fall into step behind the unlikely duo. They say nothing as they walk, but I'm sure I heard them speaking when they were first walking down the hall. My presence must be a conversation stopper.

I tend to have that effect on people.

After another minute of walking and turning through the corridor, we arrive at the double doors of the library.

Theodore stands in front of us, his back to the doors. "Are you ready?" he asks Isabelle with a wide grin.

She smiles good-naturedly and nods. "I think so!"

With a flourish, Theodore opens the door and sweeps his arms wide. "Here we are, the library!"

I hear Isabelle take a sharp inhale. I try to see the library through her eyes, as if it were my first time here. At approximately two thousand square feet, it's a marvel to behold. My father loves to read and made sure to fill each of the shelves with books for education, entertainment, and everything in between. Ornate white shelves line the walls, along with matching white shelves creating aisles through the room. In the center are three couches with enough pillows and blankets to create forts and read books in for days.

It's been many years since I've built forts here with my siblings. I'm hit with a hard wave of nostalgia but swallow it deep, deep down where Isabelle won't be able to see.

"This is incredible," she breathes.

"Are you much of a reader?" I ask.

She chances a glance at me, a faint blush coloring her cheeks. "Not really. I was already weird enough as the girl who was super into musicals."

My traitorous heart leaps at that commonality. Not that I want to share.

She sighs. "But if I'm stuck here with nothing else to do, I might as well read."

"A noble way to pass the time," I agree.

She nods, her fingers brushing the spines of the books as she walks down the aisle. "What about you? Do you read much?"

My eyes drift back to the couches, a memory of an evening here with my siblings when we first moved in. I tried to organize them into re-enacting a movie—I believe it was Transformers. As usual, my brothers were not cooperating. Henry wanted to play video games, not act out a scene. Peter insisted on being the dashing hero, instead of the minion I had assigned him to be. But little Lily, with her long, golden blonde hair... sweet Lily would do whatever I asked.

Father was on one couch, immersed in a book about business and marketing. And our mother sat on the other couch, a blanket wrapped around her legs and bunny slippers on her feet, pretending to read a book about ocean life. But I knew she was watching us with a small smile.

"Why don't you read?" I asked her.

"I'm watching my whole world," she said with a wink.

Back in the present, I snap my attention back to Isabelle, feeling my expression turn stony. "No. I don't read."

I turn away from her and walk toward the window. This is why I don't come inside the library often. Too many memories of better times. It's not the most painful room in the castle, but it's bad enough.

"Isabelle, come read me a story," Theodore says, returning to her side and pulling on her hand.

"Are there any superhero stories here?" she asks, following him to the small section of children's books. And for some reason, I follow along behind them.

He shakes his head sadly. "It's all girl books. Princesses and fairies."

"Well, a lot of times there's a dashing prince who saves the princess," she says. "I think you might find some inspiration there."

"But sometimes the princess just saves herself," Theodore complains. "Those ones are boring."

I snort a laugh despite myself. Isabelle catches the sound and chances a look over at me, and I don't change my expression quickly enough. We end up sharing a smile at Theodore's antics.

"Why are there only 'girl' books?" she asks, even using her fingers to put air-quotes around the word.

Theodore shrugs, starting to look through the options for Isabelle to read to him.

"Lily was the only one who was at the age of picture books here," I answer. "She was born right after the castle was built. Peter was already eight by then."

"So Lily is the youngest," Isabelle says, "then Peter?"

"Yes. I'm the oldest, then Henry, Peter, and Lily."

"What do they all do?" she asks.

"Henry is training to replace my father as CEO of Stone Technologies. He recently started up the gaming division of the company, which led to his engagement with Luna Jones. Peter is...off traveling the world, creating some app I don't even understand. And Lily has just been at home ever since—"

I catch myself before I can finish that sentence. I nearly said,

"Ever since Tristan Jackson ruined her life," but thankfully, I had enough sense to stop myself.

I haven't come that close to disclosing Lily's secret since... well, ever.

The enormity of what just happened hits me like a ton of bricks. What am I doing? Why am I sharing pieces of myself and my family with this stranger? What's *wrong* with me?

I swallow hard and clench my jaw. Isabelle tilts her head, unaware of the change within me.

"Ever since what?" she asks.

"Nothing." I turn on my heel and storm toward the exit. Before I leave the room, I turn back to her. "Dinner will be at six p.m. Don't be late."

I can't believe I lost my head. Something about Isabelle keeps drawing me in, but I'm determined to keep her away. From now until she leaves the castle, I won't speak to her. Not a single word. What difference would it make, anyway? She already said she won't do the movie with me. At this point, the only thing that will happen is an accidental slip of my tongue, giving her ammunition to use against me in the press.

I won't give her the chance.

Ten

ISABELLE

Three nights.

I've been here for three nights.

The snow isn't letting up. We still don't have Internet or cell service. Meaning I haven't had access to call anyone...or watch my movies.

And that also means I haven't been sleeping. I think I've gathered about three hours over the last three nights. I'm getting delirious. The voice in my head—the one whispering *outside, outside, outside*—is getting louder and louder. I don't know how much longer I can stand this.

On the second night, I thought I'd embrace my insomnia and try reenacting the "Good Mornin'" dance scene from *Singin' in the Rain*. But there's a reason why my acting goals are set on straight movies and not musicals—I have a serious lack of dance training. So I found out the hard way that doing a somersault over a couch is not as easy as it looks.

Turns out it's *not* great to stay up late. Now I've got a bruise on my shin and I still can't sleep.

All night long, I wondered what's going to happen when I get home. This movie was supposed to be my big break, the realization of my dreams coming true. Sure, it was just a cheesy rom-com on the Family Entertainment Network, but it was a LEAD ROLE. Now what? Am I going to get blacklisted by the entertainment industry for rejecting a role I was offered?

Is my dad worried? What about Jen? I was supposed to come home three days ago. I never even responded to her first message about what Adam looks like in person.

I've probably lost my job at the Cheesecake Factory, too, since I never showed up and didn't even call to find a replacement.

I'm not crying about that one. But maybe I should be, because that's the only way I'm able to pay my share of the rent. No job, no movie to look forward to... I'm lost.

I lie in bed every night, my mind racing, but I feel like I'm suffocating. Even though the castle is huge, the walls feel like they're closing in on me. I've never been so trapped in my life.

Brigette is hovering. She's super sweet, and I feel endeared to her, but even she is smothering me.

Even worse, Adam isn't speaking to me. Not a single word since he left the library—except to remind me we'll have dinner at six p.m. every night.

I've thought about staying in my room and freezing him out, since dinner is the only scheduled event we have between us, but it's almost become a game at this point. Can I get anything out of him? Even a change in expression?

So far, the answer is no.

I've said the most ridiculous things. I claimed I can ride a unicycle while juggling flames (not true). I also told him I can pick up most objects with my toes instead of my fingers (that one *is* true).

Not a single flinch.

Tonight is our fourth dinner together. I'm determined to

make him crack. My lack of sleep is making me border on absurd.

"This stew looks delicious," I comment. "Is it from Luthpaknia?"

I hoped making up a ridiculous name for a country would break him down. But I get nothing.

"The last time I was there," I continue, "I rode a flying alpaca. Have you ever seen those before?"

His eyes stay glued to his bowl.

"Of course, that was after my time in the circus. I told you about that, right? I'm a lion tamer." I tap my forehead with my index finger. "I should put that on my list of special skills... I bet it'll be useful for my next movie."

I can tell Adam is listening to every word but choosing not to react. It's time to get even more ridiculous.

"After the circus, Angelina Jolie and I opened a chicken farm. It wasn't super profitable, so we sold it to Jason Mraz."

The side of Adam's mouth twitches in a smile. I think he enjoys my name-dropping of celebrities. I take that as encouragement to continue.

"One of the hens got married to a rooster, though, and Stella Knight sang at the wedding reception. It was pretty fancy. All the roosters wore bow ties. And there were other people there, like Ryan Gosling and Tristan Jackson and—"

Adam slams his spoon down on the table. His expression instantly morphed to the most intense fury I've seen on a person's face.

Oh, crap.

Tristan Jackson.

AKA Hollywood's golden boy, the victim of Adam's fury last autumn. The unexplained secret that's been looming over everyone's heads for the last eight months.

Adam slowly turns his head to face me. "Never, *ever*, speak that name in this castle." His voice is low and dangerous, sending a chill down my spine.

"I—I'm sorry," I stammer. "I forgot—"

"Forgot what?" he snaps. "What do you know?"

"Nothing, I swear!"

He stands suddenly, his chair scratching the floor loudly. "Lionel, bring my food to my office." He stomps past me and toward the exit.

"Yes, sir." Lionel scoops up his bowl and follows Adam out the door.

I stare down at my food, too sick from nerves to eat any more. Of all the names I could have chosen, why did I say Tristan Jackson? I should have known better. That name has been running on repeat for the last four days. It's the foundation of the mystery in this castle.

I have to get out of here. But a quick glance at the window shows that the snow keeps falling. It's *got* to end soon. Because the longer I stay, the surer I am that I don't want anything to do with Adam Stone.

SINCE THIS IS my fourth night in the castle, I'm pretty familiar with the routine at each hour of the night. After dinner, I head to the kitchen and hang out with the staff. Around ten, the final few workers go to bed, so I head to my room, too. At midnight, there's a clock that strikes somewhere down the hall. And at twelve-thirty, Adam goes to bed. I know this because he slams the door of his bedroom as he leaves the office.

So now, at one in the morning, I'm pretty sure I'm the only person awake.

I'm starting to go crazy. Being stuck in here feels like suffocating. I wish I could just step outside for a few minutes, but the snow hasn't stopped.

Outside, outside, outside.

"Argh!" I cry out loud, throwing the blankets off my legs.

Maybe I should head over to the library. I can find a big nonfiction book about the Revolutionary War, and it'll be so boring, I'll have to fall asleep, right?

Would a British family even own a book about the Revolutionary War?

Regardless, I think it's the best option right now. I don't have my movies to put me to sleep, so boredom will have to be the answer. Pulling a robe around my shoulders, I suppress a shiver. I feel a sense of foreboding as I wander around the castle alone at this hour. Honestly, I could get murdered here and no one would know.

I'm *pretty* sure Adam hasn't killed anyone but...after his reaction at dinner tonight, I'm getting a little nervous that Tristan Jackson won't be on this earth much longer.

But lying in bed isn't getting me anywhere. In fact, it's making my imagination run wild. So I play my character game, embodying someone else to give me bravery.

"You are the owner of this castle," I whisper to myself. "There's no reason to be afraid of walking around your own home in the middle of the night. You have every right to go to the library."

With an inhale and a nod, I open the door to my room and escape into the hallway. I'm wearing the pink bunny slippers and too-small pajamas, but I'm not about to change clothes in the middle of the night. My feet pad quietly on the floor, but every step sounds like a stomping elephant.

I make my way to the staircase. I've been to the library a few times over the last few days, mostly to read stories to Theo and peruse the shelves. There were a few romantic comedies that caught my eye, even one by Moira Kensington, but nothing has been able to hold my interest. Right now, I'm not looking for something interesting. Boring would be preferred.

As I pass Adam's office, I notice the door is open just a crack. I halt in my tracks.

I know I'm not allowed in there. But he's asleep, right? If I spend a few minutes peeking around, just to convince myself I won't get murdered here in the castle, who could blame me? Especially after his reaction tonight, I need all the reassurance I can get.

It's crazy how fast he flips. That first morning in the library, he almost seemed...normal, at least for a moment. Despite his crazy hair and beard, it was like he was telling a friend about his siblings and family. I saw a glimmer in his piercing blue eyes that wasn't there before and hasn't been there again.

But in an instant, everything changed. His eyes turned steely, and he hasn't spoken to me since. Well, except to tell me never, ever to say Tristan's name in this castle.

"Tristan Jackson," I say out loud, a small act of defiance. I feel a smirk on my face, giving me another boost of confidence.

I place my hand on the door, pressing it open, and walk into the office. A few coals in the fireplace to my left still glow red, giving a little light to the room. I wish I had brought my phone as a flashlight, but the battery died, and I didn't bring a charger with me. Let's not forget the original plan was to stay for a few hours and then head back home. I use the faint glow of the embers to light my way, giving the office an extra-creepy vibe. Some pictures line the walls to my right—one of Adam, then, I'm assuming, each of his siblings.

I pause at Adam's picture. The picture shows him as I remember him from the movies—strikingly handsome, with dark blond hair cropped on the sides and longer on top. Piercing blue eyes that gaze into your soul. A little bit of stubble to give him a rugged look. But his expression, especially in this dark, is stern and intense.

Has he always been this way? Is this how he got the reputation of Hollywood Hothead, even before punching Tristan on the red carpet?

I move on to the pictures of the other siblings. Henry, the next brother, smiles lightly and seems pleasant. Peter's grin is a bit playful and mischievous.

I stop in my tracks at Lily. She's stunning, with her long blonde hair and sky-blue eyes. But there's a beautiful innocence in her expression, something that makes you feel hopeful.

I step back to Adam's picture, taking a moment to study him.

"What happened to you?" I whisper, wishing I could ask him that question and get an honest answer in return. I set my fingertips on his cheek, letting them linger there for a moment.

Moving on from the pictures, I notice a shelf full of trinkets next to a gigantic desk with a computer. A sliver of moonlight falls right on the shelves, illuminating a few items. There's a globe, an old-fashioned pocket watch that keeps ticking loudly, and a delicate glass red rose on a stand. I reach out my hand and gently touch the petals of the rose.

Well, apparently not gently enough. It wobbles and then topples off the shelf.

"Oh, no!" I cry out loud, bending down as quickly as I can to catch it before it hits the ground. In the process, I bump my rear end against the desk. Hard.

"Cheese and rice!" I cry out, rubbing my sore bottom with my free hand. But the important thing is that I caught the rose just in time, so I carefully set it back on the shelf.

Turning back to the desk, I notice that the computer screen is now lit up. I must have moved the mouse in the process of bumping into the desk. The light reflects off a picture frame on his desk—it's the picture I knocked down in the study my first night here, complete with the cracked glass diagonally across the image.

"Shoot, shoot, shoot," I whisper, hoping I didn't do anything to make it obvious that I was here. I scurry over to the computer screen, trying to see if I did accidentally set off anything suspicious.

The document on the screen looks boring enough, but my eyes catch on a few words.

Tristan Jackson

Lily Stone

Non-disclosure

Slander

Assault

"What are you doing here?" Adam's low, rumbling voice makes me jump and squeal.

I glance up, and there he is, standing in the doorway. With the low light and the outline of his body, I could truly believe he's a lion standing on its hind legs and not a man.

I swallow hard. How in the world am I going to explain myself to him?

Eleven

ADAM

"I said, what are you doing here?" I growl.

Isabelle's brown eyes are as wide as saucers. She bites her lip, glancing down at the computer, then back up at me. "I thought you were in bed."

I'm speechless for a moment. How is that an explanation for what she's doing here? Does she think that justifies invading my personal space? "And that gives you permission to come into my office? The ONE place I told you not to go?" I point at the security camera in the corner of the ceiling. "I get an alert whenever someone is in here. Now I'll ask one more time, what are you doing here?"

She crosses her arms over her chest. "I couldn't sleep. So I was going to read in the library, but this door was cracked open, and…" Her voice trails off and she shrugs.

My mind is spinning. The things she could have seen and done in here…it's my biggest fear.

She's going to expose all my secrets, selling them to the highest bidder.

"Who are you really?" I ask, my voice rising. "A lawyer? A

member of the paparazzi? Someone from Tristan Jackson's team?"

She furrows her brow. "No. You know that."

"You're going through my computer!" I shout, taking quick steps over to her. "The information you had access to…" I shake my head. "Don't try to convince me otherwise."

"My father is your manager," she says slowly. "You trust him, don't you? Besides, you're the one who said I needed to come up here."

I'm standing just a few feet away from her now. "Maybe Jim set me up. Everyone has their secrets."

"Not me!" She rushes over to me, closing the gap between us. Her face lights with indignation. "I swear to you, I had no malicious intention. I haven't slept for the last three nights, and I'm starting to go crazy. I just wanted to go to the library, and I accidentally knocked over the glass rose, and I bumped into the desk and—"

"You knocked over the rose?!" I can't help the panic that rises in my voice, and I run around her to the shelf, where my mother's prized glass rose sits safely on the shelf. What kind of story is Isabelle inventing? I pick up the rose, inspecting it for damages, then turn back to her. "It looks fine to me."

"I caught it in time!" she insists. The moonlight from the window illuminates her face just enough that I can see angry tears glistening in her eyes. "You don't believe me?"

"How could I? You come here just in time to get snowed in, you've been asking all kinds of personal questions about my family, and now I find you in my private office looking at sensitive documents. What am I supposed to think?" I grunt in frustration. "You need to get out of here. Now."

Her jaw sets, and her eyes are on fire. She stands in place for another moment, then says, "If you want to know the truth, then watch the recording."

"What?"

She points up at the camera. "Watch me in here. You'll be able to see that I'm telling the truth." She turns on her heel and rushes out of the room. I wouldn't be surprised if a fireball was hurled at me in the process.

I run a hand through my long hair, furious at myself for leaving the door cracked open. For trusting her. For letting her stay here, keeping her fed and warm, when all she wanted to do was expose my secrets.

And they're not just my secrets.

She could completely ruin Lily, after everything I've done to keep my sister safe.

I glance at the computer screen, a document sent to me from Bethany. It's exactly what everyone is dying to know. An explanation of how Tristan dropped the assault lawsuit against me in exchange for my silence about our financial ties and what he did to Lily.

In a way, I'd love for it all to come out. For Tristan to be exposed. But I don't want Lily to suffer the consequences. The media's attention on her would be unrelenting, and she's too fragile for that.

I sit at the desk, turning the glass rose in my hands. It looks perfect, which makes me doubt her story of dropping it even more. But, then again, she told me to watch the recording.

I set the rose down on the table and click around on the computer until I find the folder with tonight's footage in this room. It takes a few minutes to find the right moment, but eventually I see her enter the room.

She was right; the door was cracked open. I watch her take a few steps into the room, slowly turning her head and looking around. She doesn't rush to the computer, but she seems to be taking her time, observing her surroundings. The first thing she notices are the pictures hanging on the wall of me and my siblings. She pauses at each one, tilting her head to look more closely. Then she goes back to my picture and touches her fingers to my face.

Instinctively, I put my hand on my cheek, right where she placed her fingers, and feel my scar.

She murmurs something to the picture that I can't quite hear. Then she turns and walks toward the shelf of trinkets. She looks up and down at the various memorabilia my family collected over the years, including the glass rose my mother brought home for me from Paris.

"So you never forget the things we love," she had said.

And one year later, she was gone.

Just as Isabelle claimed, I watch her touch the rose, which sends it flying off the shelf. My heart leaps, but Isabelle catches it in time, bumping her rear end against the desk.

"Cheese and rice!" she exclaims, rubbing her sore spot, and I smile despite myself.

Her gaze shifts to the desk. "Shoot, shoot, shoot," she says, rushing to the computer. This must be when she realizes that the screen is on.

"What are you doing here?" I hear my own voice, barely two seconds later, low and menacing. Even I'm startled by it. I listen to our conversation, finally able to admit that I was wrong in accusing her so quickly of having ulterior motives. Not that she cowered in fear, though. She held her ground, just like Lionel said she would.

I haven't gone toe-to-toe with someone like her in years.

But again, she was in my office. Trespassing and disobeying the one rule I made while she was here. I've given her everything she could ask for, and she still snuck in.

I've seen enough. I pause the video, contemplating my next move. My eyes drift to the family photo below my computer monitor, and my thoughts drift to my mother. What would she want me to do?

Yes, Isabelle was in the wrong. But she's going to be here for some time more. Even if the storm stops, we have to wait for the snow to melt before she'll be able to drive back down the mountain. I don't want to spend the next few days miserable, feeling guilty for the way I treated her.

With a sigh, I set the rose safely back on the shelf of trinkets. I should apologize, as much as I don't want to. I exit the office and head over to her room. She said something about not sleeping, so I doubt she's asleep right now.

I knock on her door three times and wait patiently. Nothing. I knock again. Still nothing.

"Isabelle?" I say through the door, hoping my voice sounds less aggressive than in the video. "I'd like to speak with you."

Still nothing.

I try again. "Isabelle?"

"Mr. Stone?" Lionel's voice sounds from the hallway, his wiry frame dressed in a robe and holding a candle for light. "Is everything all right?"

"No," I reply, my voice clipped. "Isabelle was in my office and we got into a disagreement. I wanted to speak with her."

"Sir, she just left."

"Left?" I repeat. "What do you mean?"

"The front door opened. I received an alert on the system."

Where could she even go? It's still snowing, and her car can't make it down the mountain. I know from experience how easy it is to get lost in this forest in the snow.

My vision fills with the memory of someone else who nearly died out there. I can still feel her tiny body shaking in my arms. I can't let that happen again.

"Get my coat and my snowshoes," I say to Lionel. "I'll go find her."

CHAPTER
Twelve

ISABELLE

Outside, outside, outside.

As soon as I left Adam's office, the words got louder and louder in my head. I couldn't think about anything besides those words. More than ever, I felt the desire—no, the *need*—to get outside. I couldn't stand one more second in this beautiful prison, trapped with Adam Stone.

I ran to the front door, yanked it open, and rushed out into the snow.

Now, ten minutes later, I can admit that wasn't a good idea.

While I didn't die driving up this mountain, I'm going to die out here. In the middle of the night, in a forest surrounded by a snowstorm, with no one out here to hear me cry.

And crying is exactly what I'm doing.

I'm freezing cold, trying to pull Lily's short robe around my middle. When I first escaped, I ran as far as I could in the calf-high snow, straight into the trees around the castle. I only made it for about five minutes before I turned around and realized I was completely lost. These trees are packed tightly together, and I can't see the castle at all. I thought I could follow my footprints, but it's too dark for me to see where they are. Plus, I'm such an idiot, I didn't even put on real shoes. I'm actually wearing the fluffy bunny slippers.

Now I'm shivering, trudging through the snow, completely soaked from my knees down, with no idea how I'll find the castle.

I find a tree stump and sit down, taking a moment to rest. Now my backside is wet, too, but I don't even care. I'm exhausted, sleep-deprived, lonely, homesick, scared... The list is endless. I wish I never came here in the first place.

Maybe when the sun comes up, I'll be able to find my way. Maybe I'll have enough light to see my footsteps.

But the snow keeps falling, and I'm losing faith that I'll be able to get out of here.

My body shakes, and I'm colder than I've ever been. I'm a Southern California girl, born and raised, and I only spend time in the snow if we're taking a day trip to go skiing. Which I rarely do, and even then, I'm wearing multiple layers and covered in a waterproof jacket and pants. This is a brand-new experience, and I'm worried it'll be my last.

But...wait.

I think I hear something.

"Isabelle!"

Is that Adam's voice?

"Isabelle, where are you?" A flicker of light, its source a distance away, flashes over me.

There's no way. My heart picks up speed with the hope of being rescued.

"Here! I'm here!" I call. But my voice is too quiet, too weak from the cold.

"Isabelle!"

I try again. "Here!" It's a little louder this time, and I see the light pointing in my direction.

I summon my last bit of courage and stand, slowly making

my way toward the light. But my foot slips and I fall straight into the snow.

This could not be any worse.

"Isabelle!" Adam's voice sounds above me, and his firm hands grasp my waist and pull me to standing. "Are you all right?"

I can't even answer him. A minute ago I was sure I was going to die out here, and it feels like my brain is frozen along with my body.

I look up at him, and I must be short-circuiting, because he looks like a Viking warrior saving me from death and destruction. My breath sticks in my throat, and I'm sure I'm going to faint.

His blue eyes watch me carefully, and I'm shocked to see them soften. "You're shaking," he says.

"I'll be fine. I just need..." I choke out a sob, because even though I'm so thankful he's saving me, what I need is to go *home*. I don't want to be stuck here anymore. I want to leave this place and forget I was ever here.

Adam doesn't wait for me to finish my sentence. With one arm around my waist and the other under my legs, he scoops me up and holds me against his chest.

"Wha—what are you doing?" I manage to say through chattering teeth.

"Carrying you back to the castle," he grunts, walking through the snow in the direction he came. "You need to get dry clothes and sit in front of the fire immediately."

As much as I want to argue with him and maintain my dignity, I can't deny how incredibly nice it feels to be curled up against his chest. The warmth from his body seeps into mine, and for a delirious moment, I rest my head on his chest. Man, this guy must work out.

His head ducks to look at me. "Yes, I do work out."

Oh, my lord. "Did I say that out loud?" My eyes widen, my stomach erupting in butterflies.

Adam just smirks down at me and keeps walking.

Thoroughly humiliated, I consciously keep my mouth shut as Adam navigates through the forest and emerges at the front entrance of the castle. Half of me fills with relief at the thought of warmth, but the other half dreads the idea of being trapped there with him.

But he did come to rescue me.

And he didn't just send Lionel or one of the other footmen. He came out here himself. I look up at him, wondering why he made the effort to come get me in the snow. I guess he's not a murderer after all.

"Lionel!" he calls as soon as we enter the castle. "Get Brigette. Isabelle needs new clothes. And start the fire in the study."

"Yes, of course," Lionel replies, then rushes away.

"I'll be f-fine," I say, my teeth chattering.

"You're risking hypothermia," Adam says, his voice gruff. "Don't argue." He looks down at me, and I'm surprised again by the softness in his expression. "Let me take care of you."

I'm completely speechless. What girl doesn't want to be taken care of by a strong man? I've been sure he hates me this whole time...but maybe it's just a front.

He brings me to my room and gently lays me on the bed, where Brigette has already laid out a fresh set of clothes. She's wearing a robe and looks worried.

"I'm fine," I say weakly, and she looks even more nervous.

"Call me when she's dressed," Adam says. "I'll be waiting outside." He exits the room with heavy, dramatic footsteps.

"What were you thinking?" Brigette asks, rushing to take off my wet clothes.

I ignore her question. "I can do it myself," I say, even though I really can't. My muscles feel like they're solid, immovable.

She waves me off and continues peeling the clothes off my body. I'd be embarrassed but I'm too cold. "You could have died out there!"

"I'm well aware," I mutter. She doesn't speak anymore, just bundles me up in new clothes and slippers, but I'm still freezing.

She looks at me when I'm fully dressed, and I think she's even more nervous than before. "Mr. Stone! She's ready. Please hurry!"

He rushes back into the room and scoops me up again.

"This is really unnecessary," I protest, even though I'm frozen to the bone.

"It's really not," he replies, and he doesn't stop moving until we're in the study. He sets me down on a wingback chair next to the fire and wraps a furry blanket around me.

The fire finally seems to do something to warm me up. My whole body is shaking, but I can feel the cold start to decline.

"Your lips are blue," he says.

"I'll be okay," I whisper. "I'm starting to feel better."

He watches me, and I can tell he's debating something. After a moment of hesitation, he unwraps the blanket from around my shoulders.

"Hey!" I cry.

But he doesn't listen. Instead, he picks me up from the chair and sits on the thick, plush rug with me in his lap, wraps the blanket around us both, and holds me tightly, rubbing my arms with his hands. The combination of his warmth with the fireplace does seem to work even better, but again, I'm rendered speechless from this gentle act.

I look up at him. "Why are you doing this?"

He inhales deeply—I can feel his chest expand—and then

exhales. His jaw clenches before he decides to speak. "My sister, Lily, got lost out there once when she was five. I remember…" He swallows hard. "It was terrifying. And you've never been here before, so I knew you'd get lost, too."

There she is again. The mention of Lily is the one thing that brings any kind of softness to Adam. He's not going to say more, and he doesn't need to.

So I respond the only way I know how.

"Thank you."

CHAPTER
Thirteen

ADAM

Light begins to filter in through the window of the study, illuminating the deep red walls and paintings of trees. Despite sitting on a cushioned rug all night, my back aches. My guess is that it's around seven in the morning, which means I've been sitting here by the fire with Isabelle for approximately five hours.

After she thanked me, Lionel brought her a warm cup of tea. She drank it while I held her, ensuring her shaking subsided. Once she finished the tea, she promptly fell asleep in my arms.

She has been asleep this whole time.

I could have put her back in bed. Or in the chair. Or I could have laid her on the floor and left her.

But I can't.

I haven't held or been held by someone in years. And it feels...nice.

Ugh. I sound like my sappy younger brother, Henry.

Isabelle stirs in my arms, and I look down to see her slowly blink her eyes. When she registers where she is, she sits straight up and moves away from me. Reluctantly, I let her go, so now we're sitting a couple feet apart.

"Sorry, I..." She bites her bottom lip and darts her gaze away from me.

"You don't need to apologize. I stayed of my own accord."

She looks back at me. "Well, thank you."

I nod, acknowledging her gratitude. "How do you feel?"

"Better." She glances out the window at the falling snow and shudders. "That could have ended so badly."

"Yes." I study her, analyzing her status. "Do you need more clothes? Are you still cold?"

She shakes her head. "I feel warm enough now." She blushes, probably thinking about the fact that *I'm* the reason she's warm after her sleep.

She clears her throat. "Coffee! Can I get some coffee?"

I wave over at Lionel, who's been standing nervously in the doorway. He nods and heads over to the kitchen.

The silence in the air is thick and loaded, but I do feel the need to discuss what happened last night, especially now that she seems to be almost back to normal. After all, I had every intention of apologizing to her until I found out that she ran off. I take in a breath, preparing for the words I'm about to say. "I watched the recording."

She raises a brow. "And?"

"And...I suppose you were telling the truth. You weren't in there to intentionally reveal my secrets."

A smirk lights her face. "Told you."

I grunt, a little irritated with her smug demeanor. But I know my mother would have expected me to say the next part. "I'm sorry for accusing you."

Her face is expressionless for a moment. She holds my gaze, then says, "Thank you. I wouldn't have expected you to apologize."

I nod once, ready to move on from this part of the conversation. "But why did you go outside in the first place? You know it's snowing."

She heaves a sigh. "I'm suffocating in here. I feel so trapped. And then you were yelling at me, and—"

"I yelled at you because you were in my office. The one place you're not allowed."

"Still, you didn't have to yell at me."

She doesn't stand down, and neither do I. We stare at each other for a moment, heat passing between us.

I may have apologized for accusing her of having malicious intent, but I'm still frustrated she trespassed. "What compelled you to go in there in the first place? I've given you everything you need—a place to stay, clothes, food. The only thing I've asked is for you to stay out of my office."

Her eyes flame. "Fine. You've given me everything I need to survive. But being trapped here is terrifying. How do I know you're not a murderer?"

"What?" I ask, a shocked laugh erupting from my lips.

"You're so secretive! You won't tell me anything, not even small talk. You literally wouldn't say a word for two full days. What am I supposed to think?" She crosses her arms in front of her chest. "The door was cracked, and I took the opportunity to ease my mind. I'm terrified here, and I haven't slept in four nights. I didn't know what else to do."

"Yes, you said you were sleep deprived. Why is that?"

"Oh, I don't know. Stuck in a creepy castle with someone who looks more like a beast than a man."

Ouch.

"But it's not just that." She unfolds her arms and looks down at her hands in her lap. "It's kind of dumb."

I furrow my brow. "What do you mean?"

She fiddles with her fingers for another moment. "My mom

died when I was two. I have my sisters, but they're ten and twelve years older than me. My dad did his best to raise three girls, but I think all of our emotions were a lot for him. When I was four, I started having night terrors. He says I would wake up and not know where I was. He'd try to comfort me, but I was inconsolable. The one thing that would work was playing an old classic musical on the tiny TV in my room. *The Sound of Music* was my first one, and within minutes I was asleep. Then it was *Seven Brides for Seven Brothers, My Fair Lady, Mary Poppins...*" She shrugs. "It's become a lifelong ritual. Every night, I put on a movie and fall asleep to it. And here, with the cell service and Wi-Fi out, I haven't had that."

I swallow hard, trying to dislodge the lump that grew in my throat. Not just because I feel sorry for her, but because her story has struck home in more ways than she understands. I can't let her know what effect this connection has on me.

So instead, I abruptly stand. "Come with me."

She looks up at me, confused. "What?"

"Come. I have something to show you."

"Are you going to murder me now?" she asks, her shaky voice betraying her joking tone.

I take one step closer to her, speaking slowly. "I promise I will never hurt you. You have my word."

She holds my gaze, the tension palpable, then nods.

I turn and lead her out of the study and through the corridors, one turn after another, until we reach a room I haven't entered in five years.

"You're welcome here any time you want."

She tilts her head and furrows her brow, and instead of explaining more, I push the wooden door open and let her walk inside.

"Welcome to the theater."

Fourteen

ISABELLE

Adam calls this room the theater.

I call it heaven.

To my right, the entire wall is covered with a projector screen, offset by red velvet curtains. The rest of the room looks like the coziest movie theater in the world. There are five gray plush recliners with cup holders and little tray tables, and a step above those is a couch, big enough to sit four people comfortably, or for a couple people to stretch out and take a nap.

"This is incredible," I breathe.

"Come with me," he says. We walk between the recliners and the screen to the other side of the room, where Adam opens the door to a walk-in closet.

"This is our movie library," he says, gesturing at the rows of DVDs. "We've kept them all in case we lose Internet from storms like this one."

My mouth drops open as I start perusing the names of the movies. There are classic romances, thrillers, rom-coms... It's mind-blowing.

"You might like this section," he says, leading me to the far end of the closet. I follow him and read the names of the movies he's pointing at.

Singin' in the Rain

An American in Paris

Mary Poppins

My Fair Lady

Seven Brides for Seven Brothers

The Sound of Music

My eyes fill with tears. I press my hands to my cheeks to calm myself down, but my emotions are out of my control after the last few days.

I turn to Adam, who watches me carefully. "Sorry. I know this might seem overdramatic. But it's… This means more than you could possibly understand."

He doesn't say or do anything to acknowledge my words. But again, his eyes betray some kind of emotion… Sympathy? Pity? Understanding? I can't get a clear read on him.

I smile, trying to lighten the mood. "Why do you have so many musicals? Are you a fan, too?"

That was the wrong thing to say. His face turns stony. "No." He turns and leaves the closet.

Sigh. Another instance of Adam's sudden change in mood. I follow him back into the main part of the theater.

"You're welcome here whenever you'd like," he says. "You can even sleep here if you want." He won't look at me now, his eyes toward the exit, like he can't wait to escape.

"Thank you," I say. "Truly. For everything."

"You're welcome," he says.

We stand there awkwardly, him avoiding my gaze, before he turns and leaves the room. I can't help feeling like something has changed between us, despite his strange behavior just now. There's some kind of mutual understanding and, dare I say, respect.

I do feel bad for trespassing in his office. I also feel stupid for rushing out into the snow. That wasn't my finest moment.

With a bit of shame, I realize I never truly apologized to him for what I did. Maybe I should. He actually apologized to me, and I know I felt better after he said the words "I'm sorry."

I can't bring myself to go talk to him just now, though. He seemed upset. For now, I'll just appreciate this gift he's given me.

Even though it's morning, I'm so excited to be in this beautiful theater that I skip over to the closet and sigh happily in front of all the musicals. Which one to watch first? I pull out *My Fair Lady* and pop it into the player, then settle into one of the recliners to watch Audrey Hepburn become a real lady.

CHAPTER

Fifteen

ADAM

What's happening to me?

Isabelle is bringing out the worst in me. First, she asked questions she shouldn't have. Then in the library, she got me to talk about my family. I was able to freeze her out for a few days, but now... I actually went and saved her in the snow.

Held her all night in front of the fire.

Brought her into the most sacred room of this castle—at least to me—and told her she could come in whenever she wants.

And now, worst of all, I'm considering cleaning up my appearance.

After leaving her in the theater, I went back to my office to regroup. The computer monitor was still frozen on the moment when I entered and was speaking to Isabelle—fine, yelling at her—and it gave me another perspective on myself.

Do I really want to look like this?

What would my mother think?

Argh. I'm getting too soft.

Lionel knocks on the office door and enters. "How is Ms. Isabelle?"

"She's well," I respond, not taking my eyes off the monitor. "She's in the theater."

"Oh?"

I look up at him, his eyebrows raised. "Yes."

He presses his lips together in a small smile.

"Don't read into it," I say.

"Of course not," he says, the smile still on his face. "Is there anything you need?"

I glance down at the picture that has taken residence on my desk, then at the image on the screen. After a moment of hesitation, I finally speak the words. "Yes. Call Cassandra. It's time for a haircut."

I'M NERVOUS.

This is ridiculous. Why should I be nervous? I just got a haircut and trimmed my beard down to a more civilized length. There's nothing wrong with that.

And it wasn't for Isabelle.

It was for me.

But as I stand behind my chair, waiting for her to enter the dining room, I can't help the rush of nerves at what she's going to say when she sees me. Not only did I get a haircut, but I finally decided to wear something other than a sweatshirt and sweatpants. It's nothing too exciting, just a blue button-down and slacks, but I know she'll notice the change and comment on it.

"You look sharp, sir," Lionel comments from behind me.

I grunt in response. I'm sure he's got another smug smile on his face, but I don't want to see it.

And then she enters. She's wearing the same clothes from

this morning, her hair is a little messy, but her beauty still strikes me every time I see her.

"Sorry I'm late," she says, walking straight to her chair and not looking at me. "I fell asleep again watching movies and—oh!" She stops dead in her tracks, her eyes locked on mine. "You cut your hair."

I swallow. *Do you like it?* I want to ask, but of course I won't. That's pathetic. Instead, I just nod. "It was time."

She smiles softly. "It looks...really good."

I feel the side of my mouth start to turn up in a smile. *No, Adam. Keep it together. You didn't do this for her.* I step over to her chair, pulling it out for her to take a seat.

Slowly, she sits down as I push it in. I take a seat in my place, and the footmen bring our salad dishes.

"Thank you, Graham," she says, smiling at him.

How did she know it was Graham and not his twin... Greyson? Yes, that's his name. Greyson.

With just that small remark, I realize how well she's integrated herself here. She's not only become part of my daily routine, but she knows the staff by name, even differentiating the twins. And they know her, as well.

Just like my mother. She was so beloved by them all because she took the time to get to know each of them individually and make them part of her family.

Graham smiles at Isabelle and inclines his head.

"Yes, thank you, Graham," I add.

Graham's eyebrows rise, and I feel like an idiot. I whip out my napkin and set it on my lap. Back to Isabelle. "So, how are you feeling now?"

Isabelle takes it all in stride. "So much better," she says. "I started watching *My Fair Lady* and fell asleep right away. I've been napping on and off all day."

"And your temperature? You're not too cold?"

She shakes her head. "I'm all better." She meets my eyes. "Thank you again. I don't know what would've happened if..." She shudders. "I'm so grateful."

I nod once, uncomfortable with this show of emotion. "Will you be able to sleep tonight, now that you've slept all day?"

Why am I so worried about her? If she sleeps or doesn't sleep, why is this my concern? But I can't shake the thought of her being awake and miserable in the middle of the night.

"Even if I can't, I have plenty of movies to keep me occupied." She glances at the window. "I do wish we could go outside, though. That's the one other thing I make sure of every day. I take a morning walk and another one in the evening. It supposedly helps with your body clock. So being inside has made me extra stir crazy."

"Hopefully the storm lets up soon," I say.

She nods in agreement, and we finish our salads in silence. The footmen exchange our plates, with Isabelle graciously thanking them again, and we start on the main course. I stay silent this time. I made enough of a spectacle thanking Graham for the salad.

"So, the theater is pretty amazing," she says after a few moments of silence. "Did you spend a lot of time in there?"

I freeze mid-chew. How does she always know the exact questions to make my stomach drop?

She doesn't notice and keeps talking. "Is that where you got the idea to be an actor? I bet you watched a lot of movies in there with your—"

"That's enough," I say. "We're not discussing the theater."

She furrows her brow. "I thought because you showed it to me, I could ask about—"

"No." I say it forcefully, setting my fork down on the table with a clang. I stare her down. "You don't get to know about my personal life or my history. You can enjoy the theater as much as you'd like, but that's the extent of it."

She doesn't back down from my gaze, but meets it with her own intensity. "Fine."

We stare at each other, an unspoken battle raging between us. Who will look away first? Not me, that's for sure.

"Mr. Stone?" Lionel asks from the corner.

"Yes?" My eyes flit over to him. Ugh. I lost.

"I thought you'd like to know that the storm has ceased."

That catches Isabelle's attention. She stands without hesitation, her chair scraping the wooden floor, and she rushes over to the window. "Finally!" she exclaims, pulling the curtain aside.

I follow her in a more dignified manner, standing behind her at the window. Close, but not too close. Even from here, I can smell the lavender shampoo that she must be using.

Lionel's right, the storm has stopped. Outside, a white blanket drapes over the ground and the trees, but there's no snow falling from the sky. The sun is setting over the mountains, and the view is picturesque.

In fact, for a brief moment, I swear I can see out of my left eye. I shut my right eye, testing it out, and everything goes black.

I must have imagined it.

"It's beautiful," Isabelle breathes. She turns and faces me, her eyes wide when she realizes how close I'm standing.

Maybe I am too close.

She composes herself. "Can I go outside? I promise I'll bundle up this time. And I won't get lost."

I can understand her pull to be outside. Before everything happened with Tristan and my accident, I felt the same desire.

But now that I'm a recluse, I'd rather stay inside the castle, where the light of day can't touch my scars.

She wants to go outside, but that's still no guarantee she won't get lost. I can't risk that again.

"You can go outside," I say. "But I'm coming with you."

CHAPTER
Sixteen

ISABELLE

Twenty minutes after dinner, I'm bundled up in spare snow clothes that Brigette found in the castle. She fussed with my jacket and boots for way too long before I shooed her away. I'm ready to finally see the sun, even if it's setting.

I skip to the front door, where Adam waits for me. His haircut and beard trim look so good, it's almost overwhelming to be with him in person, instead of watching him on the big screen. And yet... I see him more as a challenge now than anything else.

He saved me. He knew I was lost in the snow, and he came for me. He held me all night by the fire, letting me sleep in his arms. He gave me the theater room, knowing I needed to sleep and understanding exactly what it would mean to me to be in there.

So yes, one minute he's gruff and rude and closed-off. But the next, he's protective and considerate. And then it's back to his default setting—grumpiness. I'm determined to break down his walls and find out why. Kill him with kindness and all that jazz.

I beam up at him, bouncing on the tips of my toes. "Let's go!"

He fights a smile, and I feel a little flutter in my chest at his response. He opens the door for me, and I take my first few steps, crunching into the snow with proper boots this time, and nearly laugh out loud. Finally, I get to be outside, and even though it's cold, I'm wearing enough waterproof gear that it doesn't bother me. Yes, I'm a Southern California girl through and through, but I can handle a little bit of cold. Especially when I've been trapped inside for days.

The snow glistens in the last bits of sunlight, while the sky is a masterpiece of colors. Orange and purple and pink streak overhead. I can feel myself becoming whole again, breathing in the clean air and seeing the setting sun.

I wander around, hearing Adam's footsteps behind me the whole time. He's giving me a little bit of space, but staying close enough so he won't lose sight of me. I wish that didn't make him even more attractive, but something about the protective alpha male totally works for me.

But he's so serious all the time. I swear, he needs to spend some time with Theo. Maybe if they played superheroes for a little while, Adam would actually have fun.

Or maybe I can have some fun with him.

"Ugh, my shoelace," I say out loud, bending down and pretending to tie it. Adam stays a few feet away from me, so he can't see what I'm doing on the ground. I work quickly, so it's not as tight of a snowball as I'd like, but I stand and whip around, throwing the ball at Adam.

And it lands at his feet.

Adam stares at the spot where the snowball landed, like he's trying to understand what just happened.

"That's...not what I was trying to do," I say, feeling warmth rush to my icy-cold cheeks.

He looks back up at me. "And what exactly were you trying to do?"

I press my lips together. "Hit you with a snowball."

"Ah." He has the decency to look amused. "I take it that sports are not your strong suit."

"Nope. I actually broke my pinky finger in P.E. in seventh grade. We were playing basketball and someone threw me the ball and...yeah. Broken pinky."

Adam shrugs. "That's fairly commonplace, isn't it? Breaking fingers in basketball?"

"I mean...it was a gentle toss. It should've been a simple catch. Even I can admit that now."

Adam takes a step toward me. "That's pretty embarrassing."

"Well, you don't have to say it like that. But yes, it is."

He steps toward me again, now about five feet away. "Maybe you'd have better aim from a closer distance."

I raise a brow at him. "Is that a challenge?"

He shrugs a shoulder. "I'm curious how bad your athletic skill really is. I won't even move. It should be an easy target."

I fold my arms over my chest. "What do I get if I hit you?"

"Excuse me?"

"I need motivation. What do I get if I actually hit you with a snowball?"

"The honor of hitting me with a snowball. I think that's a reward in itself."

I snort a laugh. "I guess striking THE Adam Stone with a snowball would be something I could brag about for years. After all, it's the same Adam Stone who had the power of fire in *Burned to the Ground*."

"True. I could just melt all the snow if we were in that universe."

I sigh dramatically. "If only. Then I could've been home already by now."

"Yes, you could." His expression turns serious. He's studying me.

I think he wants to know if I'm still angry about being locked here. But the truth is…I'm not so sure. We seem to have come to a mutual understanding, and the tone is significantly more light-hearted than before.

I'm kind of…having fun.

"Well," he says, clapping his hands together, "what do I get if you miss again?"

I snort. "There's no way I'd miss."

"I beg to differ."

"Fine." I rack my brain to come up with something ridiculous he might want. And then it comes to me. "If I miss, I'll do the rom-com with you."

His eyebrows rise sky-high. "Is that a promise?"

I nod, giving him a no-nonsense stare. "But I won't miss."

He holds up his arms. "Let's see about that."

I bend down, packing snow into another snowball. *I can't miss*, I tell myself.

But in a weird way, I wonder…do I want to miss?

Do I want to do the movie with him now?

No, of course not. He's just an interesting puzzle for me to solve while I'm stranded up here. As soon as I can get back down this mountain and home to LA, I won't think about Adam Stone again. At least not until I watch his next movie.

Once I'm satisfied with my snowball, I straighten and stare him down. He's still standing with his arms raised, a slight smirk on his face. I take aim and…

I hit him square in the chest.

"Yes!" I squeal. I start doing a happy dance, swinging my hips and turning in a circle, which is kind of tricky in the snow.

When my back is turned to him, I get smacked by something cold on my back.

I turn and face Adam, who has a mock innocent expression. "You hit me with a snowball!"

He shrugs. "What are you going to do about it?" And then he turns and runs off. Well, more like he trudges through the snow at a slightly quickened pace.

But I take my time, making multiple snowballs before chasing after him. I need to be prepared. With an aim as bad as mine, I need to have multiple attacks ready at once. After I've made five snowballs, I start following him through the snow.

It's a lot of work to run in calf-high snow, but I'm lighter than Adam and make it over to where he's hiding around the corner of the castle pretty quickly. I take aim, and my first two snowballs miss, but my third hits him on top of his head.

"Ouch!" he exclaims, rubbing his head with a gloved hand.

"Oh, no! Did that hurt?" I drop my other two snowballs and run over to him, guilt running through me.

Shoot. Did I just injure Adam Stone? Is he going to sue me?

I reach him, not sure if I should touch him or what. His face is contorted in pain, and I feel awful. Before I can make a decision, though, he hits me in the chest with another snowball that was hidden by his side.

"Hey!" I cry out.

His eyes are filled with delight.

My mouth drops open in shock. "It was a trap!"

He laughs out loud, throwing his head back. It's a glorious sight. I haven't seen Adam this happy and free the entire time I've been here. In fact, he never portrays this even in his movies. Brooding, stoic, and serious are his strong suits. But this fits even better than I would have expected. A deep sense of pride wells up in my chest, and I beam at him.

He looks back down at me with a wide smile.

"Are you making a snowman?" Theo's little voice sounds from around the corner at the front of the castle. I turn my head, breaking eye contact with Adam, but I can't see him from where we're standing.

"Theodore!" I hear Brigette call. "Get back inside this instant!"

"But I wanna make a snowman!" he whines back.

"We're not making a snowman, Theo," I call.

Adam doesn't say anything, and the levity is gone. His expression is back to its stony default. I sigh inwardly, disappointed that all my work has gone to waste.

I leave Adam's side, trudging through the snow to find Theo. Adam follows behind until we see Theo standing at the front door in his Captain America pajamas and fur-lined boots. Poor kid has been stuck inside too, and now we adults are outside having all the fun.

I point at the sky, where the sunset has turned into an inky blue sky dotted by a few stars. "It's dark now, see? But we can make a snowman tomorrow. I think the storm is over."

"I want to make a Snow Hulk," he says.

"That sounds like a great idea."

Theo looks satisfied and goes back inside. I look back at Adam. His expression is serious, unflinching. Gone are the laughs and the cheer we shared. But even still, I want to finish this occasion on a good note. "Thank you for coming outside with me. I needed this."

He nods silently. Lionel opens the door to the castle entrance and we walk back inside.

As disappointed as I am that Adam snapped back into his usual self, I saw a flicker of who he could be. And maybe who he once was. He has so much affection for his little sister, Lily. Did he ever play outside with her like this? Even from the couple of pictures I've seen of her, I can tell she has a sweet and playful personality. Surely he wanted to entertain her, too.

I head off to my room, looking forward to a warm bath, but I can't stop picturing that moment when Adam seemed like someone I'd like to know.

CHAPTER
Seventeen

ADAM

I slept horribly last night.

Visions of Isabelle, her face glowing in delight as she pelted me with snowballs—well, attempted to pelt me with snowballs—kept appearing in my dreams. In one iteration, I pulled her by the waist, her warm body against mine, and pressed my lips to hers.

I'm clearly going insane.

I climb out of bed around six, finally acknowledging I won't be able to sleep any more. Is this how Isabelle felt those nights when she couldn't sleep? I feel more empathy now, and possibly some understanding of why she thought entering my office wasn't such a terrible idea.

I slowly pace the halls, finding my way down the stairs and into my office. I figure I'll pass the time reading over the paperwork from the lawyer again.

Lionel knocks on the door. "Good morning, Mr. Stone."

"Hello, Lionel." I wave him in.

He enters, carrying my hot cup of tea. He normally doesn't bring it in until eight, but he must have heard me wake and got up himself.

"Phone service is back up," he says. "I thought you'd like to know."

"Oh, is it?" I pull my phone out of the top drawer of my desk and plug it into the charger. There's never much reason to keep it charged when the cell service drops out. I'm also not exactly dying to hear what anyone has to say outside this castle: rumors about where I am and who I'm with, or what *really* happened that night with Tristan. Perhaps Jim, Isabelle's father and my manager, will call to let me know that another sponsor has dropped out.

All things I want nothing to do with.

But thinking of Jim makes me think of Isabelle. She'd probably want to know about the cell service. I'm sure her father has been panicking since he hasn't heard from her in days now.

As I wait for my phone to boot up, I take a sip of tea. "Have you informed Isabelle yet?"

"About the phone situation? No. I figured Brigette would do it once Isabelle wakes."

I set down my tea and push my chair back. "I'll go do it."

Lionel tilts his head to the side. "Sir?"

I pause, hesitating. "Do you think it's a bad idea?"

"I—" Lionel cuts himself short, pressing his lips together in a tight smile. "I think it's a wonderful idea."

With a curt nod, I exit the office, heading down the hall to her room. But the door to her bedroom—Lily's room—is wide open, and she's not in the bed.

Ah. She must be in the theater.

I retrace my steps and walk down the stairs and around the corner, quickly pushing open the door to the theater.

As soon as I walk inside, I realize what an intrusion I've made.

Sprawled along one of the couches is Isabelle. She's lying on her stomach, her face turned toward the front of the couch. Her long, brown hair cascades behind her. My fingers itch to run through her strands, a compulsory desire to feel her, not just see her from a distance.

I ball my hands into fists, suppressing the urge. But I still take a moment to observe her beauty. She truly is stunning, even more so to me than her sisters. And while she has a fire to her, there's kindness and consideration that is absent from her sisters' personalities. Just seeing the way she treats Theo and the staff proves her heart is pure.

I smile at the bowl of popcorn lying on the ground, the one I asked Lionel to get for her last night after our snowball fight. It's empty, and I'm glad she enjoyed it.

I turn to leave, feeling awkward for entering without her approval, when I hear her stir. "Brigette?" she asks, her voice groggy.

I clear my throat and stay facing the door. "No, I'm sorry. It's me. Er, Adam."

"Oh." She pauses. "You can turn around. You've seen me asleep before."

"True." I turn to face her, and she stretches her arms high, exposing a bit of her midriff. I quickly adjust my focus to her eyes. "Did you sleep here last night?"

OF COURSE she slept here last night. Am I an idiot?

Isabelle must think so, as well. She tilts her head. "Clearly, yes."

I simply nod. We stare at each other for a moment in silence.

"So, are you going to tell me why you're here?" she asks.

"Ah. Yes. Of course." *Focus on your purpose, Adam. Stop getting distracted.* "The cell service and Internet are back online."

"Oh, really?" She stands now, and I get the full effect of her pajamas—Lily's pajamas—pink silk pants that are slightly too short but still accentuate her curves, and a silk top. "I haven't even plugged my phone in this whole time. I bet my dad has been calling and texting nonstop.”

“I’m sure he’s been calling me, as well. Hopefully he understands that nothing...nefarious happened here.”

She huffs a laugh. “We’ll see.” She starts taking a few steps toward me. “Do you have a spare charger I can use?”

She stops just a step away from me. I’m not sure she realizes how close together we are, that our chests are nearly touching. If I wanted to, I could easily take one more step, hold her in my arms, and kiss her.

What’s wrong with me? I’ve gone years without the need for physical touch, and one night of holding Isabelle has rendered me into a pathetic sap.

Maybe I’m ready for a role in a rom-com, after all.

“Adam?” she asks, jolting me from my thoughts.

“A charger. Yes. I have one. I’ll... I’ll have Lionel bring one right away.” And with that, I turn and exit the room, and not a second too soon.

Because I worry about what Isabelle is doing to me.

Eighteen

ISABELLE

What is going on with Adam?

As I walk back to my room from the theater, I can't stop thinking about him. He's hot and cold, on one minute and off the next, and when we were standing near each other, I swear he was about to kiss me. And if he had, I would have...

Slapped him?

Pushed him away?

Turned my head away?

...Kissed him back?

I shudder. No. It doesn't matter that he's devastatingly handsome. He's insulted me more than once.

But then again, he rescued me.

"Gah!" I exclaim to myself, stepping into my room.

"Is everything all right?" Brigette's voice sounds from inside the room, making me jump.

I place a hand on my forehead. "Yes, yes, I'm fine. Sorry, I didn't know you were here already."

She fluffs the blanket on my unused bed. "I'm sorry I startled you."

"It's fine. Adam just told me the Internet is back up, though."

"Oh?" She turns to face me. "That's good to hear."

"My dad is probably panicking. It'll be good to reach out to him."

"Is there...anyone else who might be panicking?"

I furrow my brow. "I mean...my best friend Jen? And maybe my sisters? Although we don't speak often."

"Mm-hmm," she hums. "Or perhaps...a boyfriend?"

"Oh!" I laugh out loud. "No. I don't have a boyfriend. No one wants to date a girl who bursts into show tunes at any time of day."

Brigette waves me off. "I highly doubt that."

"Trust me." I head over to the bed and sit with a bounce on the freshly laid covers, then wince. "Sorry. You just made that."

She plops next to me with a bounce of her own and a smile. "Tell me about dating."

I pause, thinking about my answer. The only person I really talk about dating to is Jen. My sisters don't care about my personal life, and I never had a mom around for relationship advice. But Brigette seems so sweet; it's worth a shot. "Where do I even begin?" I raise my shoulders, then let them fall. "First of all, you have to understand how impossible it is to grow up with two stunning sisters who were pursuing modeling. By the time she was eleven, Joanna already had a contract with Eleve Modeling Agency. I was born a year later."

Brigette raises her brows. "Did they pressure you to try modeling?"

"Oddly enough, no. My dad tried to protect me from any kind of show business. My mom had been the one to pursue modeling with my sisters, but she died when I was barely two years old. So my sisters continued with the contracts they already made, and my dad kept working but didn't want me to have any part of it."

"But doesn't that mean you had a more normal life?" Brigette asks.

"You'd think so, right? But it's impossible trying to date anyone when images of your sisters are plastered all over the girls' binders and boys' lockers at school. Everyone knew who my family was, even if I wasn't part of it myself."

Brigette nods thoughtfully. "But you must have drawn attention of your own. You're beautiful, kind, intelligent—"

I snort and feel my face heat, just like it always does when I'm offered a compliment. "I...not...well, anyway. Besides being compared to my gorgeous sisters, I'm a weirdo."

Now Brigette laughs. "How so? You're so poised and charismatic."

Again, another compliment that sets me off balance. "Trust me, I'm weird. You already know I can't sleep without watching movies. But that's become my life. When I'm driving, I'm listening to soundtracks. When I'm stuck in a hard situation, I embody a female main characters for strength. I've learned a little too late that being super into movies is not an attractive trait to guys." I shrug. "But it's fine. I don't need a man. And all that studying of classic movies has set me up for a great acting career." I pause, remembering I'm now stuck without any job prospects. "At least, I hope it does."

Brigette studies me for a moment. "Adam hasn't told you—"

"Ms. Lovett?" Lionel says from the doorway.

I stand and meet him at the entrance with a smile. "Good morning."

He smiles back. "Good morning. I've brought a few phone chargers for you to choose from. I wasn't sure which you needed."

I smirk. "If only the phone companies didn't keep making us switch chargers, right?" I take one from him. "Sadly, my phone is a dinosaur and I'm still using one of these. Thanks, Lionel."

He bows slightly. "You're welcome." He turns and leaves.

Excited to contact reality outside of the castle, I retrieve my purse from the closet and pull out my phone. I find an outlet by the vanity and plug in my phone, waiting for it to turn on.

"I'll let you have some privacy," Brigette says. "We'll see you in the kitchen for breakfast?"

I nod. "Thank you for talking with me."

She smiles almost a motherly grin, then pats my shoulder. "Don't count yourself out, Isabelle. You have a strength uncommon to most."

My heart tugs at me, making me wonder if these are the types of chats I've missed out on over the years.

After a few minutes, my phone powers on. Sure enough, the notifications start pouring in. I don't even bother reading them, knowing I just need to call my dad.

He picks up after the first ring. "Isabelle! Thank God! Are you all right? Where are you?"

"I'm fine, I promise. I'm still here at the castle. We got snowed in and lost all cell service and Internet."

There's silence on the other end.

"Dad?"

"You're kidding, right? Snow?"

I laugh. "Nope. This place is crazy."

He heaves a sigh. "I've been so worried about you. I even called the police."

"What?!"

"It's not like there's a national search going on or anything. I just needed to do *something*." He pauses, then continues in a hushed voice. "Are you safe? Is Adam... Do you need me to tell the police to come up there?"

"No, no, I'm fine. There's like fifteen other people here."

"You're sure? I know Adam can get hot-tempered at times."

"No, Dad. Adam has been..." I hesitate. What *has* Adam been? Rude, especially in the beginning. Angry when he caught me in the office.

But then he braved a heavy snowstorm to rescue me. He gave me the theater. And now we've developed a very tentative, cordial relationship.

A relationship sparked with attraction, at least on my end. But a cordial relationship, nonetheless.

"We're good," I finally say, unsure of how to describe the relationship I have with him.

"All right. I'm glad to hear that. So, are you coming home today?"

"Hang on." I hop out of the seat, leaving my phone plugged in at the vanity, and pull back the curtain at the window.

Snow. Piled high all around my car.

I walk back to the vanity and pick up my phone. "No way. It's not snowing anymore, but the snow hasn't melted enough for me to drive Philippe back down the mountain. And Lionel said something about the snow blowers being broken, and no plows come all the way up here."

"Hmm," he muses. "Well, I have some good news, but we'll have to work out some kinks now."

"Good news? What is it?"

"I got an interview for you with Inside Scoop."

I suck in a breath, holding back a squeal. Yes, my dad is...*my dad*, but he's also my manager, and I want to impress him. It's my first time getting my own interview for a celebrity news website, though, which is a HUGE deal. It means I'm finally getting some recognition on my own as an actress. "Really?"

"Yes. And it's supposed to be an online video conference tomorrow morning, but do you have Internet up there?"

"Adam said we did, but I'll double check. Can I do it here?"

"Yes, that should work. I told them about the movie, and it would be great if you could share that Adam is doing it with you." He pauses. "Have you talked to him about it? Did he agree to do it with you?"

"I...uh..." Well, crap. How do I tell my dad *I'm* the one who said I wouldn't do the movie now? "We kind of mentioned it but..."

"Get on it, Isabelle," my dad says sternly. He's not being rude, he's turning into a businessman. This is the struggle I see him constantly face, balancing the two sides of our relationship. And I understand. This is his job, and he wants to make sure that *both* of his clients are getting roles. "If you can make this happen, it'll be great. For both of you."

"What do you mean?" I ask. "Isn't this a step down for Adam?"

Dad heaves a sigh. "He's losing one sponsor after another. He doesn't have any other opportunities coming up. If he doesn't land a job soon, I worry that he'll be out of the scene altogether."

My eyebrows rise in surprise. "I didn't know."

"He really pulled a stunt on the red carpet last fall. I don't even know why he punched Tristan."

The words on the computer screen flash in front of my vision again.

Tristan Jackson

Lily Stone

Non-disclosure

Slander

Assault

I'm almost positive his attack on Tristan has something to

do with Lily. Nothing sets Adam into protective mode like his little sister. But it's clear that he doesn't want any of it to be public, so I stay quiet.

Dad continues. "Well, talk to Adam and let me know if you can do the interview tomorrow morning. I'll send all the details to you."

"Thanks, Dad. I appreciate you working hard for me."

"You're welcome," he says, his voice softer. He's back to Dad-mode now. "Are you sure that you're okay?"

"I promise. I've made friends with some of the staff here. Brigette is the sweetest. Did you meet her when you were here?"

"I think so," he says. "I stayed in some princess-flower room."

I laugh. "I think that's the same room I'm staying in. I love it."

"Good. I'm glad you're all right." He pauses. "I love you, Isabelle. Let me know if you need anything."

"I will. Love you, too."

We hang up, and I feel like I just got out of a huge hug. I didn't realize how much I missed my dad.

I sit at the vanity and check my messages. My hunch was correct. I did get fired from the Cheesecake Factory. I can shrug that one off, though. Then I text Jen and let her know I'm safe. Out of the corner of my eye, I notice a little ripple in my curtain.

"Brigette?" I ask.

Nothing. My heart beats a little faster. Who is in this room with me?

"Lionel? Adam?" I can hear my voice shake.

Then I hear a little giggle, and I see tiny toes peeking out from the bottom of the curtain. A smile spreads across my face.

"Hulk?" I ask.

Theo rips the curtain aside, his cheeky face grinning widely at me. "You found me!"

"Is this your secret hiding spot?"

He nods proudly.

I fix him with a serious look. "Were you listening to my phone conversation?"

He looks a little sheepish. "I did. Was that your daddy?"

I nod.

His eyes drop to the floor. "I miss my daddy."

My heart tightens for him. I haven't really thought much about how he's not even four years old, stuck here in this castle with his grandma and no other kids. "I bet you can call him, too. Have you asked your grandma?"

His face brightens, and he smiles again. "Not yet!"

"Let's go find her." I hold my hand out to him. "And after you call your dad, maybe we can build a Snow Hulk."

Theo bounces up and down excitedly. I kneel in front of him. "Now, I'm okay with you playing in here, but I don't want you hiding when I change my clothes."

His eyes widen again and he shakes his head. "Oh, no. You need pri-macy."

I snort a laugh. "That's true."

"So does Adam. I don't go anywhere that he goes."

"Smart move." Maybe I should've learned from this little kid and stayed out of the office, too.

The office.

I feel like it's still hanging between us. Is that why his moods shift so suddenly with me? Because I never actually apologized?

My dad says I can be stubborn and self-willed. He's not wrong. Apologies don't come easily for me. But I don't think they come easily to Adam either, and he was able to say he was sorry for yelling at me. Which, may I add, he *did* need to do.

That reaction was way over the top. But he's already proven his apology was sincere by treating me with kindness...or at least common decency. He's come a long way from the silent treatment and hostility he showed me the first few nights.

As I walk Theo to find Brigette, my stomach feels sick. I realize I've held out for too long, and I need to clear the air. After I pass Theo off, it's time to find Adam.

CHAPTER
Nineteen

ADAM

"It's bad, Adam," Jim says through my phone.

"Just say it," I reply.

"We've lost LuxeLife. All we have left is Verve Tech."

I rub my forehead with my hand. This is worse than I expected.

"I just got off the phone with Isabelle," he continues. "She said you haven't come to a decision about the movie yet."

I'm shocked into silence. Isabelle made it very clear that she didn't want to do the movie with me.

"But I really think this is the career move you need to make next," Jim says. "Just think about it."

I don't say anything, which isn't too abnormal for me. But this time, it's more out of confusion than disinterest in the conversation.

A knock sounds on my door.

"I'll call you later," I say to Jim and hang up the phone, setting it on the desk. "Yes, Lionel?"

"It's not Lionel," Isabelle's voice rings through the door.

My head snaps up to the door, which is still closed.

"It's Isabelle," she says.

"Yes, I figured as much," I reply.

I look around the office. Do I go out in the hall to speak with her? Or do I invite her in? I thought it was pretty clear two nights ago that I don't want her here. Why is she now knocking on my door?

"What do you want?" I ask instead.

She's silent for a moment. "I wanted to apologize."

"For what?"

"For coming into your office."

I stride over to the door and quickly pull it open. Isabelle jumps back, still in her pajamas but now with a robe pulled tightly around her waist.

I don't say anything. I cross my arms over my chest, watching her and waiting. I can't let her see how much her presence affects me.

She swallows hard. "I just want to...ugh, why are you so scary?"

My eyes widen. "I'm scaring you right now?" I wasn't necessarily trying to look scary, just...unaffected.

"Yes! You're standing there, all menacing and growly—"

"I'm not growling," I protest.

"I didn't say growl-ING. I said growl-Y. You look like you're about to pounce on an innocent little bunny."

I snort a laugh.

"Hey, there's a smile. Now it's easier." She smiles back at me, but I can read the uncertainty in her eyes. "I wanted to apologize for coming into your office. I don't think I ever said the words 'I'm sorry,' and I do recognize that what I did was wrong. I shouldn't have come in here when you specifically told me not to."

I'm stunned speechless. She has been feisty and strong-willed, attributes I actually admire in her. Which makes this apology seem even more sincere and meaningful. If I've learned anything about Isabelle over the last few days, she doesn't speak unless she truly means it or feels it in her heart.

I don't want to tell her that it's okay, though. It's not okay that she was trespassing. But all things considered, I can sort of understand why she did it.

"Thank you," I finally say. "I accept your apology. And I forgive you."

She nods once. I can see her shoulders drop in relief.

An awkward silence fills the space between us. "Did you speak with your father?" I finally ask.

She nods again. "He seemed relieved to hear from me. Apparently he even filed a police report."

"Yes, he told me," I say with a smirk. "But he reassured me that he had already called them and let them know you were all right."

"He also said that he got me an interview with Inside Scoop," she says. A wide smile spreads across her face. "It's my first one. You said we have Internet now, right? It's tomorrow morning, but I can do it on Zoom."

I fight the grin that threatens to appear on my face. Her enthusiasm is so endearing. And I remember how excited I was when I got my first interviews leading to my very first role in *Operation: Sand Dune.* "Yes, we have Internet."

"Yay!" she squeals.

I can't help it. The smile breaks free. She tracks it, her eyes lighting, but I pull back into a scowl. "Your father seemed unaware that you refused to do the movie with me."

Her smile drops and she looks sheepish. "I, uh…yeah, I didn't tell him yet."

I raise a brow at her, challenging her to admit that she's possibly changing her mind.

She rolls her eyes. "Fine. Maybe…I was a little rash to say that I wouldn't do the movie with you."

"Oh?" I lean against the doorway, my arms still crossed over my chest. "And who's to say I'd be willing to do it with you?"

She raises a brow at me, mimicking my challenging stare. "I think we both know you're desperate."

Desperate, yes.

But also...

Maybe I'm hoping to spend more time with her, even once we're free to leave the castle.

I shrug a shoulder, nonchalant. "We'll see. Now that I know it's back on the table, I have some things to consider."

"Oh, whatever." She pushes my shoulder playfully, then her mouth drops open. "Dang. You really do work out."

I open my mouth, just to shut it again. This woman knows how to steal the words from my mouth.

She holds my gaze, waiting for me to speak, but nothing comes to mind. She clears her throat and looks back inside my office. "Well, I guess I'll let you get back to it. I was going to build a Snow Hulk with Theo this morning."

I don't want to be finished spending time with her, which is the only explanation for the words I speak next. "Do you need some help?"

"Building a...Snow Hulk?" she asks, her brow furrowed.

Stupid, Adam. I seem like an overeager child. "Yes, well, I've had plenty of experience making snow animals here. I figured you could use some help."

She parts her lips, blinking a few times. It's odd, I know, but I can't help myself.

Finally, a smile lights her face, and the warmth in my chest is all the reward I need. "Yes. I'd love your help."

Twenty minutes later, our unlikely trio—Theodore, Isabelle, and myself—trudge through the snow. The weather is beautiful: clear skies with crisp, cool air. The signs show the snow melting, but it's still not clear enough for Isabelle to drive. I've never been more grateful that we don't have a snow plow up here. This storm is one of the worst we've seen in years, though.

"This is a good place for a snowman," I say, heading over to a clearing on the right, just in front of the rose garden. Hopefully soon the weather will warm up enough and my mother's favorite flower will bloom again.

"Snow *Hulk*," Theo corrects me.

"What exactly is the difference between a snowman and a Snow Hulk?" Isabelle asks.

"A Snow Hulk looks like this." Theo stands, legs apart in a squat and arms flexed down toward his stomach. He adds a loud growl for effect.

"Ah. Of course." I nod in understanding. "Why don't you start gathering a pile of snow for his legs?"

"Okay!" Theo scampers off into the snow.

Isabelle looks over at me in surprise.

"What?" I ask.

"I haven't really seen you interact much with Theo," she says. "I thought...I don't know what I thought."

"You thought I'd be annoyed by his presence and want nothing to do with him?"

She presses her lips together. "More or less."

I watch Theo in the distance, considering how much to share with her. Isabelle did just apologize for coming into the office, a gesture I wasn't anticipating. Maybe I can give her a piece of myself.

"I don't mind small children."

There. That's something.

She stands and stares, waiting for me to elaborate, and

when I don't, she shakes her head with a small smile and walks over to Theo. I follow, stopping a few feet behind her.

"Do you live close to here?" Isabelle asks Theo.

Theo shrugs. "It takes a long time to drive here. Daddy complains about the drive every time we come."

"I don't blame him," Isabelle replies.

"They live in Brookhaven," I supply. "It's just down the mountain."

"Oh, that's not too far then," she says. "I passed that town on my way. It's so cute."

"It is picturesque," I agree. "My aunt lives there, and we visit her often."

"Your aunt?" she asks.

"My father's sister. She never married and she's...well..."

"She's crazy," Theo pipes in, not taking his eyes off the snow. "That's what Mama used to say."

"Used to say?" I repeat. "What does she say now?"

"Nothing. Mama doesn't live with us anymore." Theo still doesn't look up at me, just keeps making a bigger ball of snow.

I look over at Isabelle for confirmation.

She nods slightly, stepping closer to me and speaking softly. "Brigette said his mother left him and his father, and he hasn't seen her in months."

I turn my attention from Isabelle back to Theo. A pang fills my chest at the thought of what he's going through. What a strange bond the three of us have—all motherless, but at different points in our lives and for different reasons. Theo, unlike Isabelle and myself, has a mother who decided to leave his family. Isabelle and I lost mothers who would have given anything to be with us longer. But no matter what, we all miss that critical piece of our lives.

And once again, I'm reminded that Isabelle has integrated herself into the lives and hearts of the staff. Meanwhile, I live here and can't tell the difference between Graham and Greyson.

But maybe I can change that. After all, that's what my mother did. Once the castle was built and our staff chosen, she sat down with each of them to find out about their families and their lives. It's why the employees consider this to be their home, as well, despite the fact that I don't connect with anyone —aside from Lionel. And even that is a tentative relationship.

In an attempt to take the first step, I trudge over to Theo and start building a ball of my own. "So, what do you like about the Hulk?" I ask him.

I hear Isabelle approaching behind us, then she joins in and packs snow herself.

"He's strong," Theo says. "He gets all the bad guys."

"Mm, yes," I agree. "I like that about him, too."

"He's a good protector," Theo continues. "And he gets mad sometimes, but he learns how to control it."

"That's very wise of you," Isabelle says.

"Yeah, Daddy likes Hulk. He says I can learn lessons from him. Sometimes I get mad, and Daddy says it's okay to be mad, like Hulk, but I have to learn to control the mad feelings and use it for good things instead of bad."

I keep packing snow, but I never realized how much I had in common with the Hulk. And apparently Theo, as well.

We work for the next half hour on our Snow Hulk, which proves to be more difficult than anticipated. Getting the "Hulk Smash" pose is tricky, but thankfully the snow is wet and a little more moldable than powder. When we're all done, Brigette comes outside and admires our handiwork. Theo wants to take a few pictures next to his creation while making the same pose. As Brigette snaps pictures on her phone to send to Theo's father, Isabelle and I head back inside.

"That was fun," Isabelle comments. The tip of her nose is

turning red, her cheeks glowing. She's so full of life, it's hard to be unhappy around her.

"It...was," I agree. I don't want to leave her company, though. I've been in solitude for months, and now I want to spend every second with her. "What are you doing now?"

"Getting ready for the interview, I guess? Maybe I should call my dad to rehearse with me."

"There's no need," I blurt. "I can help you."

"Oh, really? Would you mind?"

There's nothing I'd rather do, I want to say. Instead, I just shrug. "It'll be a way to pass the time."

"Okay!" Her eyes light with excitement, making my heart beat a little faster. "Let's get changed and I'll meet you in the study."

"It's a...plan," I say. I almost said "it's a date," but I caught myself in time.

Because it's not a date.

Right?

Twenty

ISABELLE

As I head back to my room to get changed, I feel a rush of nerves at practicing for an interview with Adam. I have a basic idea of the generic questions asked by interviewers, but I'm not very good at answering questions on the fly. Hopefully Adam has some suggestions that will work for *me*, and not just something he does, like look broody and stare down the interviewer until they decide to ask a different question. There's even a picture of him scowling at an interviewer that people like to use for memes of "When my boss asks me where my report is," or "When I'm ready to leave a party and my girlfriend keeps talking to people."

I step back into my room to get dressed, taking note of my phone on the vanity. It's strange, being disconnected from reality for the last few days while I've been here, but at the same time, it's actually been nice. There's been no need to obsess over social media, scrolling for hours and wasting my day. Instead, I've filled my time with Theo and books and Brigette and the staff...

And Adam.

But the screen of my phone lights up, showing me a text from my best friend, Jen. I pick up my phone and read her text.

CALL ME ASAP! I'M SO GLAD YOU'RE ALIVE!

I snort a laugh and dial her number.

"Izzy!" she squeals in my ear. "Oh, my goodness. I've been so worried. So has your dad. Did he call the police to cancel the report?"

"Yes, he did," I reply. "I'm sorry for scaring you."

"It's not your fault! I didn't even know it could snow in California in May. But I did a ton of research, and apparently that's happened in Mammoth and even Big Bear before."

I'm not surprised she did a bunch of research. Jen is a software engineer, along with her boyfriend Robby. At least that's what she tells her traditional Korean parents. But the two of them are constantly on the Internet, researching whatever they can. It's almost scary the kind of information they're able to dig up online. I feel like they should be working for the CIA with those skills—actually, maybe they are and I just don't know. She doesn't tell me much about her second secret job. But they're an adorable pair of nerds, and I love them dearly.

"I didn't know about that either," I admit. "I thought there was some kind of mystical, magical atmosphere around here." I glance around my room, still not sure that's untrue.

"Well, that still doesn't normalize the fact that you're STRANDED in a CASTLE with ADAM STONE!"

I have to pull the phone away from my ear to deal with her loud voice. "Tone it down, Jen."

"Sorry. But...girl. Tell me everything. What's he like?"

I walk over to the curtain and pull it aside, making sure Theo isn't listening in my room. All clear. "I... I don't know. It's hard to explain."

"I have time."

I laugh. Of course she has time to listen to me describe

Adam Stone in the flesh, especially after I dragged her to every one of his movies over the last few years. "Well, for starters, he doesn't look like himself. His hair was super long, and he had this scraggly beard, but it was kind of hot."

"Was?"

"Yeah. He's cleaned up now. Like Seven Brides for Seven Brothers, except even better because it's Adam Stone. Oh, and he has a scar over one eye, and I think it's messed with his vision. But we haven't talked about that." I still wonder where that came from, because he didn't have it a year ago, or even when he was on the red carpet and punched Tristan. But it doesn't seem like a scar from that event. More mysteries to solve.

"Did he clean up for *you*?" Jen asks suggestively.

The thought has crossed my mind. I never asked him why he chose to do it right after he saved me from the snow. But I wouldn't dare say that out loud. "I don't know. When I first got here, he was extremely rude and condescending. He said I was only up for the role because of my dad."

Jen gasps. "What a jerk!"

"Don't worry, I told him off."

"You didn't."

"Oh, I did. I told him I wouldn't do the movie with him, tried to leave, and realized I was snowed in. So that was a little awkward."

Jen giggles. "I bet."

"But he put me up in his sister's room, and the staff here has been super sweet and welcoming. Then he gave me the cold shoulder for a few days—I still don't know why—and then I snuck into his office and he got mad so I ran outside in the snow, but he rescued me and—"

"What in the world?" Jen interrupts. "Is this real life?"

"I'm not totally sure," I admit. "It feels like a fairy tale.

Anyway, I hadn't been sleeping. You know my thing about watching movies before bed. And with no reception or Internet, I couldn't turn my mind off. Well, it turns out he has this incredible in-home theater, and a huge collection of movie musicals. So I've been hanging out and sleeping in there the last few days."

"And Adam? Is he...still rude?"

I hesitate. Because yes, he is still rude...sort of. A little gruff and closed-off, like he's worried that I'm going to see too far past his exterior. But I've seen sides of him that are making me fall.

Hard.

"I'm not sure how to describe it," I say softly. "But I feel like there's something there."

"Something?"

"I can't explain it." I sigh. "So I'm not sure about the movie anymore. I feel like we're starting to understand each other." I smile to myself. "He's even been asking the staff to leave bowls of popcorn for me in the theater."

"Oh, how scandalous," Jen says with a silly voice.

"Hush, you."

"I'm teasing. It's actually adorable."

I shake my head, wanting to move away from this conversation. "Anyway, I have exciting news. I have an interview tomorrow morning."

"No way! Who is it with?"

I put the phone on speaker and check the text from my dad. "Inside Scoop. My dad just sent me a zoom link for tomorrow at nine-thirty."

Jen hums, and I know her well enough to know she's thinking something but not saying it. "What?"

"Don't get your feelings hurt," she says. "But why are they interviewing you? You've done a few commercials and that role with one line in *Whispers of Deception*, but I didn't think that was interesting enough for an interview with Inside Scoop."

Ouch. I mean, she's right. But I was so excited about the prospect of being interviewed that I didn't consider that part of it.

"I'm sure you'll do great," she says quickly, filling my silence. "Forget I said anything. What do I know about Hollywood?"

"You know everything I tell you," I say.

"Exactly. Nothing of my own. So if you didn't think anything of it, then it's going to be awesome."

"Adam offered to coach me."

"See!" She laughs. "Although I'm not sure his style of interviewing will work for you. The silent, brooding, grumpy-face memes won't serve you as well as they do him."

"True, true," I laugh. "I'll take his advice with a grain of salt."

She laughs again and sighs. "Oh, I miss you. I can't wait until you come home. Do you think it'll be soon?"

"I'm not sure." I glance outside again. "The snow is still piled high, and it's pretty cold. But if the storm stays away, it'll probably be just a few more days."

"Keep me updated. We'll get dinner and you can tell me all about the castle and Adam. I have a feeling...never mind."

"What? You can't leave me hanging like that."

She pauses. "Something about the way you're talking about Adam makes me think... I have a feeling you'll be coming home with a new friend."

"Okay," I say, drawing out the word. Yeah, I could see that. "I guess we're kind of friends now."

"Mm-hmm," she muses. "And is that all?"

"What do you mean?"

She groans. "Come ON, Izzy!" Her voice rings through the

room, still on speaker. "It's Adam Freaking Stone! You've dragged me to every one of his movies for the last five years. And now you're stuck in this castle with him, fighting and playing in the snow and I'm sure the tension is building and building—you're going to kiss him, I just know it!"

"Jen! There's no way I'm kissing Adam Stone!"

"You know you want to."

"Oh, my lord." I rub my forehead with my hand. "A kiss has to be two-sided, you know."

"And with your gorgeous looks and amazing personality, I'm sure there's a mutual attraction going on."

I blow through my lips. "You've known me for fifteen years. There's no 'gorgeous looks' going on here, just an awkward, average looking, movie and musical obsessed nerd with two model sisters. If anyone's kissing Adam Stone, it's one of them."

"Your shallow, self-obsessed, narcissist sisters? Yeah, no. Anyone who's been around your family knows you're the catch. Not them."

"Well, thanks." This conversation, once again, reminds me why Jen is my best friend. We went through the awkward middle school years together, and she helped me find my own strengths in high school, taking me out from the shadow of my sisters. When I told her I wanted to pursue acting, she cheered and has been there to support me every step of the way.

"Any time." I hear her fingers clicking on her keyboard. "Hmm, it doesn't look like he's dated much recently. I can do some more research and find out if you're his type."

"Don't use your illegal tech skills for this!"

"Who says it's illegal? I mean...fine, whatever. Just go make out with Adam and tell me how it is."

I gasp. "You're impossible."

"Isabelle?" Adam's voice sounds through my doorway. "Are you ready?"

"IS THAT HIM?" Jen calls, her voice still on speakerphone. "HE SOUNDS SO HOT!"

I immediately hang up the phone, not even bothering to say goodbye. She's going to pay for that later. "Heyyy, Adam."

His head pokes around the open door. Why did I leave my door open? And why isn't he just waiting in the study for me? "All ready?"

"Almost. You, uh, didn't hear any of that, did you?"

He blinks, impassive. "Hear what?"

Oh, thank goodness. "Nothing." I paste a big smile on my face. "Let me freshen up and I'll meet you in the study?"

"Sounds good." He turns and leaves, and I fall backward on my bed, praying Adam didn't hear me talking to Jen about kissing him.

CHAPTER
Twenty-One
ADAM

I overheard Isabelle's phone conversation.

I don't feel good about it.

But in a way, I feel *very* good about it.

I'm not patient when it comes to Isabelle, and she was taking longer than I expected to arrive in the study, so I went to check on her and...maybe eavesdropped more than I should have.

Isabelle's friend, Jen, kept saying that we should kiss. I think I like this friend of hers. And apparently, Isabelle has been "dragging" Jen to every one of my movies over the last few years. Isabelle never seemed like a fawning fangirl, but maybe she knows how to keep her composure. Or maybe I really did frighten her when we first met. Either way, I'm flattered.

Isabelle didn't say anything about wanting to kiss me, but if her friend's words were any indication, she wouldn't be opposed. And she didn't say that *she* didn't want to. Just that she didn't think *I* would want to.

Well, I do.

More than she knows.

Jen's comments about Isabelle's sisters were interesting, as well. She called them shallow, self-obsessed, and narcissistic. From the few interactions I've had with them, I'm not surprised to hear those descriptors. Is that what I expected from Isabelle, as well? Is that why I was so rude to her in the beginning? Granted, in general, I've always been more...let's call it 'direct.' I don't see the point in dancing around everyone's feelings. I know what I want, and it's quicker to get there right away.

But Isabelle won't take that, and I respect that even more. She's challenging me to be more considerate.

Like my mother.

Lionel is right; no one has challenged me since my mother passed away. I miss her dearly—the reason why I won't spend much time in the theater—but Isabelle is filling some of the gaps her loss has created.

The more time I spend with her here in the castle, the more I realize I want to spend time with her outside the castle, as well.

Isabelle enters the study, wearing another of my sister's dresses. It fits her frame, showcasing her curves, but the length hits an awkward spot on her calf. I only know this because Lily has her dresses custom-hemmed to touch her ankles. Her feet are covered in bunny slippers, which make me smile more than I should.

"You should have the tailor make you a dress," I say in greeting. "I'm sure you'd enjoy wearing something that actually fits."

She looks down at her dress. "Does it look that bad?"

"No," I say quickly. "But a dress that fits you properly would be more enjoyable."

"I guess." She shrugs. "It's not like I'll be here for a long time. But it would be a cool memento to take home with me."

A pang hits my chest at her mention of leaving soon, but I

just nod. "Speak to Brigette and let her know to have the tailors meet with you."

"Sure." A sly smirk fills her face. "I need an occasion for this dress, though. Maybe you should bust out a tux and we'll have a party."

She's teasing, but something about her makes me want to play along. "Maybe we will."

She grins, then takes a seat next to me in the other wing-back chair in front of the fire. "So. What are you thinking as far as interview prep?"

"Well, you never know for sure what these interviewers are going to ask. But there are a few basic answers you should have prepared, and many times you can spin their questions back to those answers."

"Interesting." She straightens in her seat. "Well, I've got all my favorites ready to go. You know, color, season, food–"

"Hang on, hang on," I say, unable to hold back the laugh that erupts. "You're not interviewing with Teen Beat, are you?"

"Uh...I don't think so."

"Unless you're a seventeen-year-old heartthrob, it's unlikely that you'll ever be asked what your favorite color is."

"Oh." Her eyes flit down to her hands, and I feel a bit ashamed for making her doubt herself. She needs confidence right now, not embarrassment.

"But let's warm up with those questions for fun, hey?"

One side of her mouth lifts in a grin. "Sure."

Her grin warms my chest. "All right, let's try again. So, Isabelle, what's your favorite color? And why?"

"I love yellow. I love anything that has to do with the sun, especially since I take a walk every morning and every evening. Yellow, like the sun, makes me happy."

I nod. Not bad. "And your favorite time of day?"

"I love mornings. The day is always so full of possibilities.

Evenings are difficult for me, you know. Wait, I probably shouldn't say that in an interview. That's a little embarrassing."

"And that's why we're practicing," I say. "You want to figure out your boundaries for public information. Some celebrities don't even share their true favorite color, they just make something up to keep their entire lives private."

"Huh. Interesting." She shakes her head. "I think I'm happy to share some pieces of my reality. My favorite color doesn't seem like an invasion of my privacy. But other things, like watching movies every night, is a little too...intimate."

But I know about you watching movies every night, I think. I get to know some of those personal parts of her.

I change the subject. "What's your middle name?"

Now her whole mouth lights with a grin. "It's Rose."

"Oh." And now I can't stop my mind from turning. Rose, like my mother's favorite flower. Rose, like the figure she almost broke in the office. Rose, like the flowers that grow outside this castle in the summer.

Our eyes lock, the moment charged, as she watches me process that piece of information. I feel unusually vulnerable in this moment and decide to break it with some levity. "Is that made up, or is that the truth?"

"Truth." She doesn't seem uncomfortable, more curious at the reaction she elicited in me.

I gather myself, ready for another question. "How about... nicknames?"

"Well, my best friend, Jen, calls me Izzy. That's been my nickname growing up." She pauses. "But I found out recently my mom called me Belle."

I furrow my brow. "How did you find that out?"

She bites her lip. "Off the record?"

I nod in confirmation.

"I was going through my dad's garage recently, trying to

find some of my old yearbooks, and I found my baby album. A picture of me and my mom fell face down on the ground, and I saw my mom's note on the back. 'Belle is six months and waves at everyone she meets.' I started pulling out more photos, and they all had my mom's looping handwriting on the back, detailing what I was doing. 'Belle is seven months and tried avocado for the first time.' 'Belle is nine months and has started fake crying so I'll hold her.'" She has a wistful smile on her lips. "I guess we should have known I'd be an actress."

"But your father never told you?"

She shakes her head. "I never knew that was her nickname for me."

I swallow. "Belle," I say, almost a whisper. "It suits you."

She holds my gaze, the moment charged with meaning. I clear my throat, looking down at my hands. "So, uh, tell me when you decided to finally pursue acting as a career."

Her shift to professionalism is impressive, almost as if she were expecting me to ask this question. "Well, my dad is a manager for actors. I've been around Hollywood my entire life, and even though he tried his hardest to keep me from wanting to act, it's like a pull I couldn't resist."

"What specifically pulled you to acting?"

She twists her lips to the side of her mouth. "I've lived my life in the background. My two older sisters have been professional models for as long as I can remember, and I've always just been...there. But my imagination is one of my strongest traits. So instead of wallowing, I'd sit in the corners, imagining I was a princess surveying my kingdom, or a peasant girl watching the aristocracy, and I'd fully embody that character, immersing myself in this imaginary world. It's become a game I still play. When I got into high school, I realized that what I was doing was acting. And after college, I decided I've waited too long to live the life I deserve. I've been practicing my whole life for this career, and it's been a journey to get here."

I'm stunned speechless. Her heartfelt expressions are pieces of her soul, entering into my mind and drawing me to her in ways I haven't felt with others before.

But she misinterprets my silence. "Too much? I should've known to say something less personal."

I swallow hard. "A little, yes." She's right. That story, while enormously impactful to me, is too personal for an interview. "You could just say you always loved playing pretend as a little girl, and it's become part of you."

She nods. "Is that what you say in interviews?"

"More or less." I narrow my eyes at her. "Well, you should know. Haven't you seen my interviews?"

"Oh, I don't really follow much of what you do." But her eyes betray her words, not meeting my gaze and darting around the room.

"Mm-hmm," I muse. "Well, typically I say that I've always loved movies and stories, and once I got to an age where I could pursue my own interests, acting came naturally."

She raises a brow, looking directly at me. "But that's not the whole story."

I shake my head. "No."

She waits patiently, biding her time. "So, what is the story?"

She shared a piece of herself with me. It only feels natural to return the favor. "Growing up, I was always the one in charge of my siblings, responsible for keeping them in line. The best way to do that was to put on plays. I'd assign each of us a role— naturally, I was the dashing hero—"

"I would expect no less," she says with a smile.

I incline my head to her. "And then we'd perform these plays for my mother. Her eyes would light up and she'd always give a rousing standing ovation."

"But you didn't want to act when you were younger? You waited until, what, five years ago?"

I nod. "It was…" My voice trails off. I haven't spoken this next part out loud. But Isabelle waits patiently, and I swallow down the pang. "After my mother died, I realized I didn't want to do what was expected of me. She would have loved to see me act, but I was too worried about my father's and siblings' expectations. I was supposed to be the one to take over Stone Technologies. My father had been training me my whole life for it. But when she passed, I just…left."

It's the first time I've spoken specifically about my mother's passing to Isabelle. She doesn't flinch; perhaps she already knew. And she lost her mother, as well, although hers was at a much younger age. But it's a bond we share, the thread we shared with Theo earlier, one that is uncommon to most.

Isabelle places her hand on mine. I look down at our joined hands, but the warmth I feel can't be seen. For the second time, I feel like my left eye is starting to see again. I blink a few times, keeping my gaze on our joined hands, trying to determine if my sight is back without looking like a maniac.

"I'm glad you decided to act," she says, breaking my attention. "But I'm sorry for the circumstances that led to it."

"Thank you," I say softly.

She sits back, taking her hand with her. I want to reach out and hold it again. I want to touch her, to feel her near me. After months of living here, cutting myself off from most human interaction, I want to fill my senses with Isabelle. But I fear it's too much.

And, apparently, I was wrong about my eye. It's still dark.

"I thought I was supposed to be the one getting interviewed," she says with a small smile, lightening the mood.

"Yes. I'm sorry about that." I rub my forehead. "I don't know what came over me."

"Don't apologize," she says. "I have a feeling you needed to get that out."

I look over at her again, warmed by her nonjudgmental attitude. Her kindness slowly melts away my icy exterior, and the more time we spend together, the more time I *want* to spend with her.

And I need to know if she feels the same.

Twenty~Two

ISABELLE

Adam shifts in his seat. "All right, back to questions about you."

"Let's go," I say.

"One thing they might actually ask is your favorite movie." He tilts his head, a smirk on his lips. "I'm sure you'll say it's *Quantum Directive*."

I raise a brow at him. "I have no idea what you're talking about."

"Come on. Surely you took your friend to see that one. Even I admit that it was one of my best films."

I suck in a breath. "You did overhear my conversation with Jen!"

His eyes widen when he realizes his mistake. "Just bits and pieces," he confesses.

I rack my brain, trying to remember at what point in the conversation Jen talked about making out with Adam, and if that was before or after she LOUDLY announced I had dragged her to every one of Adam's movies over the last five years.

Yikes.

Better to just move on, unaffected. "I may have seen *Quantum Directive*, but it's not my favorite movie."

"But it *is* my best film," Adam says, leaning toward me.

I shrug a shoulder. He's not wrong. Not only was he ridiculously handsome in his black suit, but he was intelligent, charismatic, flirtatious... My cheeks flame just thinking about how Jen and I squealed in the theater when he finally kissed the female lead.

Aaaaand now I'm thinking about kissing Adam.

"*Seven Brides for Seven Brothers*!" I say, quickly shifting the conversation back to my favorite movie.

He sits back in his seat. "Really?"

I nod. "I know it's got misogynistic overtones, what with the brothers all kidnapping the girls and making them fall in love with them, but the music and the dancing..."

"Is Adam your favorite character?" he asks, teasing.

"Ew, no," I laugh. "It's Ben for sure. The winter scene is..." I make a chef's kiss gesture. "Besides, Adam just disappears and leaves everyone alone while he broods in the cabin."

Adam's expression sobers, and I realize how strange it is that this Adam in front of me did exactly what Adam in the movie did by running away from his wife and brothers.

I clear my throat. "But nothing compares to that barn raising scene. The dancing is absolutely incredible."

Adam gives me a small smile. "It is."

I tilt my head at him. "Wait, so you've seen it? I thought you didn't—"

"Next question," he interrupts, any hint of a smile completely vanished.

Just when I think I'm getting somewhere with him, he completely shuts down. I keep getting glimpses of who he is under his stony exterior, and it feels like someone I could bond with. But now he's all business.

So we talk about other favorites. No, not raindrops on roses and whiskers on kittens, but favorite foods (his is filet mignon with a blue cheese crust, mine is beef wellington, which I don't get to eat very often) and favorite places to be (his is the snowy mountains, mine is the beach in Hawaii).

Lionel comes in as I'm describing the cliff overlooking the ocean by the seven sacred pools in Maui. "Mr. Stone, your aunt is calling."

"Agatha?" He furrows his brow, then stands. "I'll take the call—" He cuts himself off, looking at me, then sits back down. "Actually, I'll take the call here. She can meet Isabelle."

Lionel bows his head and leaves to get Adam's phone.

"Agatha is…interesting," Adam says to me. "But I think she'll provide some entertainment for our evening."

I'm about to ask what he means, but Lionel comes in with Adam's phone, and my jaw drops at the sight on the screen. An elderly woman…dressed as a pirate wench, complete with an eye patch.

"Hello, Aunt," Adam says, a small smile on his lips. "You've chosen an interesting ensemble."

"Yes, you should try the eye patch," she says, her thick British accent tinging her words. "It's partly inspired by you and your injury, after all. I'm not sure how you function, being unable to see through your eye."

Adam clears his throat, visibly uncomfortable. So he *is* blind in one eye.

Agatha takes it all in stride. "I'm so glad I'm able to get through to you. Was your cell service cut off again?"

"Yes, it's been snowing."

"In May? Ah, you must have been in quite a foul mood."

Wait…was Lionel telling the truth about the weather being dependent on the resident's mood?

No way. That's too silly.

"But you must be happier now," she continues. "And no wonder, since you've got a beautiful woman next to you. Who are you, my dear?"

"Oh! I'm Isabelle Lovett," I reply.

"Lovett? How do I know that name?"

"Her father is Jim Lovett, my manager," Adam supplies.

"Ah, yes. He's to blame for Adam leaving us for Hollywood."

"Aunt," Adam protests. "It's not his fault I left."

"No?" Agatha retorts. "Perhaps if you had a different manager, you wouldn't have stayed there and come home sooner. But no, you had to instantly book a movie and become a big success." She wiggles her fingers around her head and rolls her eyes at the screen, and I laugh.

"I'm glad you think my father is good at his job," I say.

"Hmph," Agatha replies. "So, what are you doing there? I didn't think Adam had any visitors these days."

"Well, we're possibly going to act in a movie together," I say.

Adam turns his head to look at me. "Are we now?" he says softly, and his eyes twinkle with...hope?

I shoot him a glance. "It's the easiest explanation, isn't it?" I whisper back.

"Speak up, dears!" Agatha calls out. "None of these side conversations."

I chuckle and turn back to her. "I came up to meet him and happened to get snowed in, so I'm stuck here until it's safe to drive back home."

"Ah." She watches me carefully, and I feel like she's assessing me, trying to determine if I fit some criteria. After a few moments of silence, she claps her hands. "Well! I'm glad to hear that. I won't keep you any longer. Enjoy your evening!" And she promptly ends the call.

"She's...interesting," I comment.

Adam snorts. "Yes, she definitely is." He pauses, a wistful look in his eyes. "She has a soft spot for Lily."

I nod but stay quiet. I've realized that when he brings up sensitive subjects, it's best for me to let him express himself at his own pace and not to prod him with any more questions.

He changes the subject back to interview tips, helping me plan out my general approach and personality traits, but before long, I'm yawning. "Sorry," I say. "It's not you, I promise."

He smirks. "I'm highly offended."

"I'm sure you are."

He stands, then holds his hand out to me. "Come. Let's get you to bed."

I put my hand in his, surprised by his gentlemanly propriety, and feel the warmth from his touch travel from my hand and into my belly. He wraps my hand around his arm, just like a gentleman, and we walk together out of the room.

"To the theater?" he asks.

I just nod, and we walk the rest of the way in silence. When we reach the door, he stops and turns to face me.

What's happening right now? Do we hug? Shake hands? Kiss?

No, no, no Isabelle. No kissing.

"Thank you for your help," I finally say. "I feel so much more prepared now."

"You would've been fine without me," he replies. "But it's always better knowing what you're getting into."

I give him a small smile, and he leans down, pressing a sweet kiss on my forehead. I suck in a breath at the contact of his lips on my skin. It's just a kiss on my forehead, but it sends sparks down to the tips of my toes.

"Sleep well...Belle," he says.

I look up at him, and he has uncertainty in his eyes, like he's wondering if he crossed a line using the nickname from my mother.

It's the exact opposite. My eyes feel wet, and my face fills with a huge grin. He smiles back at me, and if he wanted to kiss me, I think I'd let him.

But instead, he just nods, releases me, and leaves.

Oh, Adam Stone. What are you doing to me?

Twenty~Three

ISABELLE

I wasn't able to sleep well last night, even with my movies. If anything, the movies and all their romance made it worse.

All night, I've been replaying my conversation with Adam and remembering the look in his eyes when he talked about his mother, or the feel of his lips gently touching my forehead. I could hear his voice calling me "Belle," warming my heart.

I'm twitterpated by Adam Stone.

I spent most of the night watching movies and drifting in and out of sleep. These couches in the theater are ridiculously comfortable. At six thirty, I return to my bedroom to get ready, and, as usual, Brigette is there.

"Good morning, Ms. Isabelle!" she chirps.

"Good morning, Brigette," I reply. "I have to get ready for my interview this morning."

She claps her hands together in delight. "May I please do your hair?"

I tilt my head side to side, figuring she might as well. She's been begging me every morning since I got here. "Sure."

She jumps in the air and rushes over to the vanity, faster

than I expected her to be able to move. "I thought you'd never agree!"

With a laugh, I follow her lead and sit in the chair at the vanity. She starts brushing my hair, meeting my eyes in the mirror and smiling at me.

"I never had a daughter," she says.

"No?"

She shakes her head. "Two boys. And they've given me wonderful grandsons, but no girls to spoil. Even when Miss Lily was here, her mother was the one who would do her hair. I've always wanted a little girl to pamper. I have four sisters, and we used to do each other's hair all the time."

"Four? And I thought I grew up in a house full of girls."

She laughs. "There were five of us. My poor father. But it taught him a lot about empathy."

"Wow." We sit in silence for another couple of minutes, as she plugs in a curling iron and starts sectioning out my hair.

"Don't worry, I won't do anything extravagant. But I'm an expert with a curling iron."

"I believe you." And I truly do. I was hesitant before, but maybe I should've let her give me a makeover when I first got here.

"So, you and Mr. Stone seemed to have a nice conversation last night," she says, a teasing lilt in her voice.

My cheeks flush red, completely visible in the mirror. "We did."

"It seems that you've developed a...friendship?" She keeps her focus on my hair, making it easier for me to think and respond.

"I think so. He's a lot less closed-off, which makes it easier to talk to him." I look up at her. "Has he always been so..."

"Intense?" Brigette supplies.

"I was going to say rude, but sure. Let's go with intense."

She smiles softly, winding a piece of my hair around the iron. "Mr. Stone has always been *intense*. Serious, almost to a fault. As far as rude, he's battled that side of himself since childhood. Perhaps a better word would be 'blunt.' But his mother would encourage him to temper that side of himself with empathy." She sighs. "And while she was alive, it made a difference."

"And after she died, he just stopped trying?"

She shrugs a shoulder. "It seems that way. Mrs. Stone was the heart and soul of the family. When she passed, each of the children took it in their own ways. Unfortunately, Adam became more selfish and neglected all of his siblings and his father. He ran away from his family's expectations so he could pursue acting."

"What about his siblings?" I ask, wanting to get a fuller picture of the family.

"Henry seems to have handled it in the healthiest way. He took over where Adam left, filling his role as second in the family company. Peter has embraced his childish side and is trying to live life to the fullest, traveling and forgoing all responsibilities. And Lily," she puts a hand over her heart. "Lily desperately needed the guidance of a mother."

The words from the document on Adam's computer flash in my mind again. Was there something between Lily and Tristan Jackson? Is that what made Adam go crazy?

I'm about to open my mouth and ask, but Lionel knocks on the door. "Ms. Isabelle? Mr. Stone wanted me to ask where you would like to have the camera and computer set up for your interview."

Flutters erupt in my belly, knowing that Adam was considering what would be best for me. "Oh! I hadn't really thought about it."

"Mr. Stone suggested the dining room. Would that be amenable to you?"

"Yes. Thank you."

He nods and turns out of the room. I look back at my reflection, blushing cheeks and all, hoping Brigette doesn't notice.

But she totally does. With a sly smile, she says, "I think a certain someone is encouraging Adam to think of others besides himself." She winks.

"Who, me?"

"Yes, you!" She laughs out loud, releasing a section of my hair from the clip and starting on the last pieces of my hair. "Mr. Stone is intense, but that also translates to fierce loyalty and protectiveness. When it comes to the ones he loves, there is nothing he will not do to ensure their safety and happiness. It's why his mother's death broke him. He couldn't save her. And despite the fact that she died surrounded by the ones she loved, he felt that there was no reason to attach himself to anyone anymore, not when they would just leave him in the end."

Her words sink in, and my heart breaks for him. "How sad."

Brigette nods. "But there's something about you that's bringing him back to life. You challenge him, but you're also patient with him." She runs a wide comb through my hair, separating the curls. "I have hope for him now."

She fluffs the hair around my shoulders, and my eyes widen at her work. "Brigette! You're incredible! Why didn't I have you do my hair before?"

She shrugs, a little shy now. "I can do your makeup, as well."

I nod enthusiastically, and for a moment, I wonder what Adam will think when he sees me all made up.

Half an hour later, I'm sitting in front of the computer in the dining room, ready for my interview. I'm wearing the outfit I wore on my first night here. If it was good enough for meeting Adam, it should be good enough for an interview.

I haven't seen Adam this morning. I had hoped that he'd come by to give me some well-wishes, a little extra boost of confidence, but he's nowhere to be found.

I swallow down my disappointment. That's okay. He helped me prep last night and sent word through Lionel this morning, and that means more than he'll know.

A window pops up on the screen, saying the host has joined the meeting and will let me in soon. I inhale and exhale deeply, channeling my inner Audrey Hepburn. I can be poised and collected, answering their questions with grace. I study my appearance on screen, thrilled with Brigette's work. Now I want her to do my hair and makeup every day. And my looks are only part of it—the conversation with her fills an empty space in my heart I didn't know was missing.

The screen changes and I see a brunette woman smiling at me. Her chin-length hair and dark lashes look familiar—I've seen her interviews online before.

"Hi, Isabelle! I'm Allegra," she says warmly. "Thanks so much for joining me today!"

"Thank you for having me!" I reply with a big smile.

"I'm not sure if you've seen our interviews on Inside Scoop before, but we'll have a few video clips spliced together, and there will be a written article summarizing our conversation. Do you have any questions?"

I shake my head, eager to get started.

"All right, let me start recording." She clicks on her mouse, and an alert appears that the meeting is being recorded. "So, Isabelle, let's start with an easy one. What was it like growing up with sisters who are professional models?"

"Oh." I wasn't expecting to talk about my sisters right off the bat, but I guess it's a basic question. And, thankfully, one I prepped with Adam. In truth, it wasn't the best. It made my sisters shallow and self-absorbed, and I was just along for the ride. But in reply to Allegra, I say, "It was really exciting! I got a glimpse of life behind the cameras. And every time they were printed in a magazine or commercial, I was able to show it off to my friends at school."

"That's so cool. I bet you made a lot of friends that way."

Yeah, fake friends. "Yep!"

"That's great. Did your sisters have any pets growing up?"

What a weird question. "No, we didn't have any pets. Catherine has really severe allergies, so even though she wanted a dog, she could never have one."

"Oh, that's interesting! I don't think anyone has reported on her allergies before."

Shoot. Was that supposed to be a family secret? No one ever mentioned it before.

Allegra continues. "Now, your sisters have said often they make sure to eat full, well-rounded meals, which is so admirable for models these days. Where did that influence come from?"

I blink a few times, unsure what these questions have to do with me and my acting. "I'm sorry, I must have missed something. What is the focus of this interview?"

She furrows her brow. "Your manager didn't tell you?"

I shake my head, dread filling my stomach.

"It's an article series about celebrities told by their closest family members. We're getting the inside scoop from you on your sisters."

Her words sink in, and I feel a sting behind my eyes. *I will not cry. I will not cry.*

This has nothing to do with me, or acting, or my own career.

It's all about my sisters.

My heart hurts, but I can't let her know. Even if this interview isn't about me, I can do my best to present myself in a way I'll be proud of. One day, when I'm an A-list actress and people search my name, I don't want anything online that will embarrass me.

Maybe I can still spin it in a positive direction. I can throw in a few references to my own acting career, and then she'll have to ask about it.

I nod, recalling the question she asked. "Well, I think my sisters' respect for nutrition came from our mother. From what I've heard, she was an amazing cook and always kept my dad and sisters well-fed. I'm glad they have that reputation in the modeling community."

"Do you go to a lot of their shows now?"

Bingo. Here's my opportunity. "Unfortunately, no. I've been busy with my own pursuits lately, building up my own career as an actress. But I have some exciting projects on the horizon."

"That's nice." Allegra doesn't even bat an eyelash. "When's the last time you saw your sisters?"

I press my lips together, trying to remember while swallowing down the disappointment that this article will not go in my favor. At all.

I'm about to open my mouth and answer when a pair of strong arms appear at my sides, hands resting on the table in front of me. Adam's voice sounds above my head. "Isabelle doesn't have much time to see her sisters because she's preparing for a movie role with me."

Allegra stares for a moment, and I can see the recognition wash over her face. "Is that...Adam Stone?"

I tilt my head up to look at him, wondering what in the world compelled him to do this.

CHAPTER
Twenty-Four

ADAM

I swore I wouldn't interfere. Then why in the world am I doing this?

I know why. I've been standing outside the dining room door, listening to Isabelle's interview, and fuming at that "reporter" for only wanting to know about her superficial sisters. Isabelle was so excited last night to have her own interview, to have the spotlight on herself for once, and this couldn't have been further from the truth.

I waited as long as I could outside the door, even hearing her try to spin the conversation in her favor, but when Allegra didn't cooperate, I knew I had to intervene.

Maybe this is stupid. No one has seen my face in months, and no one knows about the scar over my eye, since that happened just a few months ago.

But if I know Hollywood, nothing will get the attention back on Isabelle like my sudden appearance, directing the spotlight to her.

Isabelle looks up at me, her big brown eyes filled with shock and gratitude, and that's all I need to see this through.

I look back at Allegra on the computer. "Hi, Allegra. Yes, it's Adam Stone."

Allegra's mouth drops open. She's at a loss for words. "How...what..."

"Nice to see you, too. I'm glad Isabelle is getting a chance to interview with you."

"Where have you been for the last year?" Allegra finally manages a full sentence.

"That's not important. What is important is the upcoming movie that Isabelle and I will be starring in. She's an incredible actress, and everyone will know her name in the coming months. I suggest you take advantage of the opportunity to be the first reporter to break the news about our upcoming movie." I move out of frame of the camera, looking back at Isabelle. Her eyes fill with joy, and a beaming smile lights her face. I might have to deal with public backlash for this, but Isabelle's reaction makes it all worth it.

"Um, okay! So, Isabelle, tell us about this movie," Allegra says, recovering.

"Yes, so...hang on one second." Isabelle mutes herself and turns off the camera. "Can you sit over there?" she asks me, pointing at the seat across from her at the table.

I furrow my brow. "You want me to stay?"

She nods. "It'll help me feel like I'm just talking to you instead of being interviewed."

I fight a smile and walk around the table, taking a seat across from Isabelle. She nods and turns the microphone and camera back on. "Sorry about that. The movie is a rom-com, and it's going to be produced by the Family Entertainment Network." Her eyes find mine, and she smiles as she talks. I don't fight my smile anymore. I grin back at her, and we have our own conversation. And I realize, somewhat unfortunately, how utterly enamored I am with this woman.

❉

AFTER DINNER THAT NIGHT, where Isabelle and I have a lively conversation about the merits of *Quantum Directive*, we go to the study for an after-dinner drink. Our evening together last night filled a place in my heart I didn't know I was missing, and I want to spend as much time as possible with her now. She's sitting on the floor, flipping through a book about the Revolutionary War she found in the library (she told me not to ask why), and I'm sitting in my wingback chair, reading *East of Eden*. I feel like the vision in my left eye is coming back, and I'm trying to subtly test it by shutting my right eye and assessing what I can see. Some light comes through, but it's still too blurry to see clearly.

That's progress.

Isabelle suddenly looks up at me. "I think Josephine has a thing for Lionel."

I'm thrown by her sudden conversation. "Josephine...the seamstress? And Lionel?"

She closes her book and sits on her knees. "When I met with Josephine this afternoon to get a dress made...that's still okay, right?"

I nod. "Of course."

"Lionel brought me over to her room, and she was *so* flustered. She dropped a bunch of pins and was all flushed. Lionel was even smiling at her. I think he likes her back."

"Are we in middle school?"

"Oh, come on, Adam! It's so sweet! You can't be such a grump that you're not a *little* smitten with the idea of older people falling in love."

Ever my savior, Lionel comes in with two hot cups of tea.

"Thank you, Lionel," I say. I keep an eye on him, not sure what I'd see that would magically tell me he's in love with

Josephine. But now that Isabelle put the idea in my head, I can't let it go.

I also wonder what Isabelle's dress will look like.

"You're welcome, sir." Lionel sets the tray down on the side table then straightens. "Mr. Lovett just called."

"Called me?" I ask. "Or Isabelle?"

"He called the main castle line and asked for either one of you, saying that he had called your cell phones but neither of you responded. I told him you were both occupied and would call back as soon as you were available."

I look over at Isabelle, wondering if she's as reluctant to call him back as I am. These moments with her are magic, and I don't want to leave this bubble. But real life awaits, and it's time to face it.

She nods and turns to Lionel. "Can you bring my phone here? We'll call him together."

Lionel inclines his head with a smile at Isabelle. "Of course."

He leaves the room, and Isabelle turns to me. "Do you think the interview is already online?"

"Probably." I heave a deep sigh. "Showing my face may not have been the best choice. They'll want to break the story as soon as possible. But I wanted to help steer the conversation away from your sisters."

"Thank you for that," she says. She looks down at her hands. "I can't believe I thought the interview was for me. Of course it was for my sisters."

"No. It's not your fault." I slide down from the chair and sit next to her on the floor. "And you deserve to have the spotlight on you. You're going to have an amazing career as an actress."

Her big, brown eyes look up at me, pinching something in my chest. "You really think so?" she asks, so earnest.

I nod slowly, not breaking her gaze. "I do."

I'm not sure which one of us moves closer, but now our

arms are touching. The heat from her body radiates into mine, but she keeps her eyes on me. I pivot slightly to face her, lift my hand, and run my fingers up her arm, reveling in the softness of her skin. She sucks in a breath, and my hand reaches her shoulder...then her neck...then wraps around the back of her head.

She knows what's coming, and she's not telling me no.

I lean in, our lips just a breath away. Her nose brushes mine, and I can feel her breath on my lips. Slowly, I bring my lips to hers, a feather-light touch against my mouth, and—

"Here you are, Ms. Isabelle!" Lionel enters the room.

We break apart like two kids caught in the closet. Isabelle scrambles to her feet, and Lionel's eyes widen comically. Once he realizes what he just interrupted, a smirk appears on his mouth.

Thanks, buddy.

Isabelle takes her phone from Lionel. "Thank you. We'll... call my dad. Right now."

I narrow my eyes at Lionel, but he just winks at me and walks away. "Let me know if you need anything else," he says in a singsong voice as he exits the room.

Isabelle stares at the phone in her hand, as if in a daze. After a moment, she comes to and looks down at me on the floor. "So...I guess we'll call my dad?"

I sigh. "Sure. Let's call your dad."

Twenty~Five

ISABELLE

What I really want to do is kiss Adam. Like, a for-real kiss. Because that tiny brush of our lips wasn't enough.

Not even close.

But the moment has been broken, and now we need to face reality. I could probably look up the interview myself, but for some reason, hearing about it from my dad will be an easier pill to swallow than watching it and cringing.

I sit on the floor next to Adam, still feeling the waves of chemistry buzzing between us even though I'm not touching him anymore. I dial my dad's number and put it on speakerphone.

"Isabelle!" his voice rings through the room.

"Hey, Dad," I say. "Adam's here too. You're on speakerphone."

"Hello, Jim," Adam says, his rich voice rumbling in my chest.

"Oh, good. It will be easier to talk to you both at the same time. Have you seen the interview yet?"

"No." I suck in a breath. "How is it?"

"It's creating quite a buzz. Adam, you should've let me know that you were going to make an appearance."

"I wasn't planning on it," Adam says. "But when Allegra was only focusing on your other daughters, I needed to steer the conversation back to Isabelle."

"What do you mean?" Dad asks.

"Didn't they tell you what the interview was for?" I ask.

Dad pauses, just long enough for me to question his next words. "No. They just said they wanted to interview you."

"Jim, come on," Adam says, his voice hard. "You're an experienced manager. You must have known that they weren't interviewing Isabelle for herself. They wanted an inside story on her sisters."

I glance over at Adam, filled with gratitude. I'm not used to being defended like this. When it comes to my family, my sisters always had the limelight, and I was pushed aside. Now, having my dad as my manager creates friction that wasn't even there before. But having Adam stick up for me is a new sensation, and probably means more than he'll understand.

"Fine," Dad says, his voice sharp. "I knew. But I wanted Isabelle to get a chance to practice interviewing before it was her turn. I didn't expect you two to turn it into a viral marketing scheme."

"That wasn't my intention," Adam says, rubbing his forehead with his hand.

"Well, that's what happened. You haven't been seen since you were on the red carpet of the Goldies, and now you show up with Isabelle and your scar on full display for the world to see." Dad lets out a loud breath. "But it's not bad. There's a lot of speculation about the two of you. And while I have my reservations, as Isabelle's father, a fake relationship between the two of you wouldn't be bad for publicity."

"What?" I squeak out.

"Absolutely not," Adam says firmly at the same time.

I narrow my eyes at him. "What's wrong with being in a fake relationship with me?"

His mouth drops open, then he shuts it. "It's not... That's not what I..."

"You two can discuss it," Dad says. "But my phone is ringing off the hook. Everyone wants a statement about what the two of you are doing together. And pulling off a fake relationship wouldn't be hard, given the way you two were making googly-eyes at each other."

Oh, my lord. I do not need my father commenting on my "googly-eyes" at Adam. Especially not after we barely kissed, and that was for real. Now he wants us to be in a fake relationship?

My head is starting to spin.

"We'll discuss it," Adam says, filling my silence. "But we'll look at the article first."

"Sounds good," Dad says. "I'll text Isabelle the link now." He pauses for a moment. "Isabelle, take me off speakerphone. I want to speak to you privately."

I hit the button and hold the phone up to my ear. "Is everything okay?" I ask.

"I wanted to ask you the same thing," he says. "Are you all right? Are you being treated well?"

I smile. Once a dad, always a dad. Even though being my manager has complicated our relationship, I'm grateful that his heart is in the right place. "Yes. I'm doing great, actually. Adam even coached me last night for the interview."

"He's not being too rude?"

I look over at him, his eyes full of curiosity and concern, words I never would have used to describe him when we first met. "Not at all."

"Good. Hopefully the roads clear in the next couple of days and you can leave that place."

A few days ago, I would have agreed. But now, being here with Adam feels safe. The beautiful prison has turned into a refuge, a haven from the prying eyes of Hollywood. And I realize...

I don't want to leave.

And it's all because of Adam.

"I'll get in touch tomorrow," Dad says. "Have a good night."

"Bye, Dad," I reply. I hang up and look at the phone in my hands.

"Is everything all right?" Adam asks.

I look back up at him and nod. "He just wanted to make sure I'm okay."

Adam pauses for a moment. "And...are you?"

I hold his gaze and smile. "Yes."

The side of his mouth lifts in a grin, one of the few I've gotten from him over the last week.

My phone buzzes in my hand, and I shift my focus down to the screen. A text from my Dad comes through with a link. "Here we go," I say, opening the message and clicking on the article.

The headline reads, Adam Stone Makes His First Appearance in Months!

Below is a screenshot of Adam looking straight into the camera. I've been cropped out.

I scroll down to the text, where the article mostly talks about Adam's appearance, the fight he got into with Tristan, and the mysterious scar over his eye. Which is still a mystery for me, too. The last paragraph of the article finally mentions me.

Adam will be appearing in a movie with Isabelle Lovett, younger sister of supermodels Joanna and Catherine. The rom-com will release on the Family Entertainment Network, a far cry from Adam's typical action movies. Release date TBD.

Underneath is a screenshot from the interview, where Adam is standing above me and I'm looking up at him, like he's my everything.

No wonder my dad says we could make a fake relationship work.

But that's it. That's the only reference to me, even though I talked to Allegra for twenty minutes about my path to becoming an actress.

So much for an article about me.

"I'm so sorry," Adam murmurs next to me. "I didn't mean to take all the attention away from you."

I shrug my shoulders, brushing it off. "It's all right. You were just trying to spin it in my direction."

"But it still didn't give you the focus you deserved." His hand runs down my arm. "I wasn't thinking."

I look down at where his hand rests, wrapped around the soft skin inside my wrist. An apology from Adam means so much, especially considering where we started. I look back up at him, his eyes filled with concern. "It's okay."

I'm disappointed, but probably less than I would have been if he hadn't stepped in. Because then the article would've just been about my sisters and nothing about me at all. At least this way there's a small buzz going about my connection to Adam.

He stands. "Come with me."

I furrow my brow. "Where?"

"To the theater." He runs a hand through his hair, looking like he needs to brace himself for what he's going to say. "Let's watch something to take your mind off of all this."

I stand and laugh. "Don't look so excited. You don't have to watch something with me."

"It's not that," he says. "I actually...don't mind your movies. I used to watch them, more than you probably expect."

"Oh?"

He swallows. "The theater was my special place with my mother. We would watch movies together after all my younger siblings went to bed." He smiles again, this time a little sheepish. "Classic musicals were our favorite."

My mouth drops open. "That's why you have so many of them!"

He nods. "But I haven't been in there since she passed."

"Oh." My giddy mood turns into something a little more somber. This is a big deal for him, for multiple reasons. Not only is he willing to go back to the room that meant so much to him and his mom, but he's sharing this with me and telling me about his experience with grief. He hasn't said much to me about her yet other than last night when he explained that he went into acting after she died. And now it makes even more sense—it was something special that he shared with her, and he wanted to continue to feel her presence in some way.

I exhale and take him by the hand. "Let's go. But you get to pick the movie."

CHAPTER
Twenty-Six
ADAM

Isabelle doesn't let go of my hand as we walk to the theater, and I don't want her to. She pulls me into the movie closet and waves her hand at the musicals section. "Pick."

I look at her, noting how small this closet feels after our barely-kiss. I can imagine pushing her up against the wall and kissing her senseless, knocking DVDs off the shelves…

Focus, Adam.

I don't have to think hard about my choice. I pull *Singin' in the Rain* off the shelf and hand it to her.

"The ultimate classic," she says with a smile. She lets go of my hand and heads back to the main room.

I guess she's not having the same fantasies that I am.

She puts the movie in the player and settles on the couch, patting the spot next to her.

"By the way, thank you for my popcorn," she says.

"Do you want some now?" I ask, starting to stand.

She pushes me down. "No, I'm good. Let's just watch the movie."

We settle into the couch and watch Gene Kelly explain his

entrance into the world of acting, laughing at his lies and marveling at his dance moves.

"That's how it was for you, right?" she asks, bumping her shoulder into mine.

I smirk. "Oh, yes. Lots of singing and dancing."

"Seriously, though. You didn't have to tough it out? At all?"

I shake my head. "I know I'm fortunate in that way."

"Well, it seems like it went to your head."

I turn my head sharply to look at her, and she has a devious smile on her face. "What is that supposed to mean?" I ask.

"You know." She rolls her eyes. "You have this reputation of getting whatever you want, and it's definitely not because you're so sweet."

"Fine. That's true." I cross my arms over my chest, irritated that she's taking this in such a negative direction.

She puts a gentle hand on my bicep. "I didn't mean to offend you. I'm just trying to put the pieces together."

"What pieces?" I ask, the movie long forgotten now.

She shrugs a shoulder. "You're a mystery," she says. "I know you have your secrets—and I won't push you to tell them to me —but I'm just trying to understand where you came from and why you are the way you are."

I unfold my arms, but she keeps her hand where it is. "And how would you describe the way I am?"

She twists her lips. "Broody."

"Broody!" I exclaim, insulted. "Like a hen?"

She laughs out loud. "Maybe the word is brooding. Mysterious. Brusque. But when you let your guard down..." She focuses on me. "Generous. Considerate. Protective."

Each word tightens my chest, knowing that she's seen past my stony exterior. Of all the words she could use, she chose the ones that hit at my core desires, especially when it comes to Lily.

"I wish that were true," I finally say.

"It is true," she insists. "I've seen it... It's the way you act with me."

Her brown eyes blink with innocence, but there's so much more to that sentence than she understands. Because I don't let just anyone see this side of me. I don't let my guard down with just anyone. I would blame it on our forced proximity here in the castle...but if I'm being honest, it's Isabelle. The pull between us is undeniable, and it would be even if we were somewhere else. But maybe I wouldn't have the opportunity to feel this tether between us if we weren't stuck together. I thank the snowstorm for the opportunity to get to know her and connect with her.

The movie continues in the background, but neither of us pays attention to it. Our eyes are locked on each other, and I feel a desire to tell her everything about the last eight months. Everything that has been weighing on my heart, a burden I've had to bear for nearly a year.

The way I've disappointed my sister and let her down, and my determination to never let her go through anything like that again.

I pick up the remote and pause the movie. "What I'm about to tell you is private," I say. "I can trust you, right?"

She nods slowly. "You can."

I let out a breath. "Then I'm going to tell you exactly what happened last fall with Tristan Jackson and my sister, Lily."

CHAPTER

Twenty~Seven

ISABELLE

I'm aware how monumental this moment is. Warmth wells in my chest, knowing that Adam has found enough of a reason to trust me now, and I resolve to do nothing to break his trust in me.

"Tristan and I were close friends," he begins. "When I started acting, he took me under his wing and taught me all about the industry. I'm sure you're aware he was a child star."

I nod. I watched him on the Disney Channel as a kid.

"It worked well for a while. He introduced me to producers and directors, helped me make friends, and took me to the cool parties. But it all fell apart. A year in, he encouraged me to make some awful financial decisions—decisions that benefited him and his friend James Hook. There was some stupid app his friend created that he wanted me to invest in, and like an idiot, I listened without doing my own research." He rubs his forehead. "I lost everything. And when I confronted Tristan about it, he literally laughed in my face. That was the end of our friendship."

"But Tristan seems so..." I hesitate.

Adam narrows his eyes. "Kind-hearted? Hollywood's golden

boy? Yeah, he's great at deceiving everyone. It's why he's such a good actor."

Adam's words make me pause. Is *he* acting with me, too? Is this all practice for the movie we're supposed to do together?

But it can't be. He's sitting here, telling me about his personal financial issues, and we haven't even gotten to the part about his sister yet.

"How does no one know about Tristan's behavior?" I ask.

"Because I'm the one who made the bad decision," he says. "Technically, he's not at fault. He's sneaky like that."

My sense of justice flares like fire. There are few things I hate more than bad people who get away with terrible things. And I have a feeling we're not done.

"That was a few years ago. I've done my best to stay away from Tristan and not make any new friends in the business. I do my job—and I do it well—but I don't make relationships with anyone and stick to myself. It worked out well. Until..."

"Until the Goldies," I fill in.

He nods. "I was taking pictures on the red carpet, and Tristan sidles up to me, throwing his arm over my shoulder like we're best friends again. He's smiling for the cameras, and I'm... not."

I snort a laugh. He's being honest; he rarely smiles for pictures on the red carpets. It's not in his personality to fake a smile, and I kind of love it.

"But under his breath, he starts telling me that he's been getting close to my sister Lily, who was barely eighteen at the time. And he tells me details about her that no one would know unless they had really talked to her. I knew he had her in his clutches."

A sick feeling twists in my stomach. Lily, the baby sister he always wants to keep safe, was in love with his worst enemy.

"Then he tells me that she's going to meet up with him that

night to run off and get married in Vegas, and I—I just snapped." Adam exhales. "I punched him in the face."

"As you should have!" I exclaim. "He totally had it coming."

He gives me a half-grin, and my heart flutters despite itself and the serious conversation. "He did. But that didn't give me the result I hoped for. I was seen as the instigator, and I got thrown in jail while Tristan ran off. With Lily."

I gasp. "She went with him."

He looks down at his hands, and the hurt in his eyes kills me. "She did. I called Henry, my younger brother, to bail me out of jail and start the search right away. As soon as I was out, we headed to Vegas. It wasn't easy, especially while trying to keep the situation out of the public eye, but we did it."

"Did they get married?" I ask, worried about the answer.

Adam shakes his head. "No. I don't know why he postponed the actual wedding, but they weren't married when we found them in Vegas. We found their hotel room, knocked on the door, and Lily was alone, so she opened it. When Tristan came back, it was almost like he expected us to be there. When Henry waved a check in his face in exchange for sending Lily home and never contacting her again, Tristan didn't hesitate to accept." Fury fills his expression and his fists clench. "He made Lily pack her things with tears streaming down her face; he was just smiling with his arms crossed over his chest."

My mouth drops open. "What a snake!"

"No kidding." He runs a hand through his hair, and I can tell he's trying to calm himself down. "We took Lily back home and got her settled back in Silver Lake City, and I came here to the castle to hide out until everything blew over. We called our cousin Bethany, who's a lawyer, and she got the ball rolling on all the legal agreements to make Tristan drop the charges against me."

"Yeah, how exactly did you manage that?" I ask.

"My silence in exchange for him dropping the charges," he says with a sad smile. "So no one will know how much of a scumbag he is."

I furrow my brow. "Is that a fair exchange?"

"What do you mean?"

"He's just going to do it again, if he hasn't already! How many girls will he take advantage of before he gets taken down?"

"I...I don't know," Adam admits. "I was just thinking about protecting Lily."

"Doesn't Lily want him to face the consequences?" I ask.

Adam shakes his head. "At first, she was completely devastated and kept telling us that they were in love, that we were wrong, and that we'd never understand what they had between them. After a few days, especially after Henry and Luna got together, she slowly realized that she had been manipulated and he never cared for her after all."

"And now? Isn't she angry?"

"Yes," he says slowly. "But she's not in any state to come forward about what happened to her. She's still very fragile."

I nod. I can understand that. If someone had claimed to love me then threw me away for a check, I'd be broken, too.

Adam shakes his head. "Besides, if she came forward, Tristan would retaliate for sure, whether against her personally or using the paparazzi against her. And she's made it very clear that she wants nothing to do with fame." He looks away for a moment. "Well, that kind of fame."

"What do you mean?" I ask.

"Lily was studying to become a professional pianist. She could have done it, too. She's an incredible player and performer. But when everything happened with Tristan, she pulled out of all her classes and studies and has been staying in the family penthouse apartment in Silver Lake City."

"Wait, so she doesn't leave at all?"

"No. It's for the best. She needs to be kept safe."

I twist my lips to the side, a little unsure about the way Lily has been locked up. But maybe she really is that fragile and broken and needs time to recover. Who am I to say how she should or shouldn't react?

But anger still simmers in my blood. "So Tristan just gets to keep living his life, pretending like nothing is wrong, when we know he's done this to an innocent girl."

"I suppose so," Adam says. "I haven't really looked at it that way."

"Something has to be done," I insist.

Adam's expression darkens. "Don't get yourself involved," he says. "That's not why I told you about this."

"I know." I pause a moment, taking a step back from the heat of the moment and the story he's told. "Why *did* you tell me?"

He holds my gaze a moment, but it's not awkward. He's thinking about how to communicate his words properly, and I like that about him.

He looks down at his hands. "I've been alone for a long time," he finally says. "And I don't just mean here in the castle. I mean alone, like how I live my life." He looks back up at me. "But with you here, I don't feel alone anymore."

"Why, because I'm sneaking into your office and taking over the theater?" I ask, a smile on my lips.

He doesn't return the smile. "No," he says quietly. He shifts to face me with his whole body, lifts his hand to my face, and cups my cheek. "Because you're sharing my life with me. And I didn't know how much I needed that until now."

I swallow hard, feeling the weight of his full attention on me.

When I first got here, Adam's intensity was frightening. I put on a brave front, forcing my way through our interactions.

But now? His intensity burns a fire in my soul, and I'm pretty sure an inferno rages within him. But all I want to do is stoke the flames of these fires, not put them out.

"You make me feel human again," he says. "I just..." He doesn't finish that statement.

He leans in, crushing his lips to mine, and kisses me.

I was right about the inferno. Adam kisses me with a fire I've never felt before. Passion and emotion pour out of him. He holds my face gently, but his lips move with fervor and desire. I keep pace with him, wrapping my hands around his neck and digging my fingers into his hair. He uses his other hand to pull me close, and our kisses finally slow to something softer and sweeter.

"I don't want to be your fake boyfriend," he says, low and soft.

His words surprise me, especially considering the way he's been kissing me. "No?" I ask, my voice breathy. "Why not?"

"Because I don't want anything fake with you."

My heart melts at his words. "So, what do we do instead?"

He gives me another half-smile. "I can think of some things we can do for real." And he dips his head down, kissing me again.

"No, seriously," I say with a laugh, pulling away from him. "What do we say—publicly?"

He sighs and leans his forehead against mine. "I'm not sure. I've never liked sharing my personal life." He leans back and looks into my eyes. "The snow is slowly melting. In a few days, we'll have to leave this place and face reality. Can we just...stay like this for a few more days? Enjoy each other and what we have, and ignore the fact that there is anyone out there wanting to hear from us?"

I smile. "That sounds perfect."

Twenty~Eight

ADAM

Isabelle and I spend the next few days soaking in each other's company, refusing to check our phones or acknowledge the outside world. We eat breakfast together, go out in the snow and build snowmen with Theo or have snowball fights, warm up by the fire in the study, and watch movies. Lots of movies. We argue over the best parts of the Sound of Music. She says it's the dance scene, I say it's when the captain joins his family on stage to sing "Edelweiss." We agree to disagree.

Oh, and there's lots of kissing.

The snow is melting, and with it, we know the clock is ticking down with the remaining time we have left in our bubble. The snow on the road is still thick enough that Isabelle can't make it down in her little car, but it's only another couple of days before that excuse disappears.

We're sitting in the theater, Isabelle in my arms, as we watch *The Phantom of the Opera*. She agreed to take a slight break from her classic musicals for the sake of one of my favorites.

"I know the phantom is a major red flag, but..." Isabelle's voice trails off.

I turn to look at her. "Feel free to finish that sentence."

She smiles up at me. "He's hot." She presses a quick kiss to my lips. "And he reminds me of you."

"Is that so?" I ask with a smirk. I won't admit this to her, but I've always felt a kinship with the phantom. Not that I'd groom and kidnap the girl I'm obsessed with, but the loneliness and darkness feel familiar. "You're not into Raoul?"

She wrinkles her nose, an adorable gesture. "He's so...meh."

I chuckle. I'm about to ask her more of her thoughts, but Lionel knocks on the door.

"Yes, Lionel?" I say.

"I know you're avoiding your calls, but your sister is requesting to speak with you."

I stand immediately, rushing over to the door to take my phone from him. Lily's face is on the screen. "Lily? Are you all right?"

"I'm fine!" she replies. "I've been texting you and getting no response. I want to know all about this girl you're holding hostage in the castle."

Isabelle laughs out loud.

"Is that her?" Lily shrieks. "I want to meet her!"

I walk with the phone over to the couch and hold it so Lily can see us both.

"Hi, Lily!" Isabelle says. "I've heard so much about you."

"And I know NOTHING about you!" Lily replies. "Since I don't have any Internet access." She narrows her eyes at me. "Because *someone* thinks I can't handle it."

I narrow my eyes right back at her. "It's not just my decision. How did you even find out about Isabelle, then?"

"Agatha called and told me about this girl at the castle. And then Luna showed me the interview when she came to visit with Henry. We're both dying to know what's going on. We're shipping you guys."

"Shipping?" I ask.

"They want us to be in a relationSHIP," Isabelle explains.

"Ah. That's...ridiculous," I reply.

"Don't get hung up on the terminology," Lily says. "Are you guys...you know...romantically entwined?"

"Blech, that's even worse," I say.

"But yes," Isabelle says.

I turn to look at her, my brows raised. "So we're publicizing this now?"

She shrugs and presses a kiss to my cheek. "It's just your sister."

"Awwwwww!" Lily claps her hands in delight. "I never thought I'd see the day my biggest grumpy brother would fall in love!"

I freeze. "I—uh—I wouldn't say—"

"Oh, hush," Lily says. "You two are in love and there's nothing you can say to convince me otherwise."

I turn to check on Isabelle. Is she as alarmed by this "love" claim as I am? No, she just looks amused.

I watch her address my sister. "Lily, Adam told me that you play the piano."

Lily gives a sad smile and shrugs. "I'm working on a few pieces."

"I'd love to hear you play. Would you play something for me?"

"Really?" Lily perks up. "I haven't gotten to perform for anyone new since Luna first came to visit."

"Really," Isabelle says. "I'd love to hear."

Lily props the phone up against the table and we see her hop over to the piano. I click the mute button so Lily doesn't hear our conversation. "Thank you for doing this."

"Of course," she says. "I feel for her. But...she doesn't seem as broken as you make her seem."

The first few notes of the piano come wafting through the speakers of my phone. I watch my little sister, her long blonde hair flowing down her back as she furiously hits the keys on the piano. "She does seem much better," I admit.

"Maybe you should ease up on her," she says gently.

The first feeling that flares up is irritation, my natural inclination when anyone says something that contradicts my instincts. And when it comes to Lily, my instinct is to protect her. To keep her away from anyone and everything that could ever hurt her.

But holding Isabelle in my arms calms me, and I take a moment to consider what she says. Maybe Lily isn't as broken as I thought she was. Maybe it's time to start letting her out of the penthouse.

"I'll talk to my father and brother," I reply.

Satisfied, Isabelle settles back into my arms to listen to Lily's performance. Lily has improved even more than I remembered. She probably spends all her time in isolation practicing and improving, which I didn't think was possible at her skill level. She finishes her piece, and I unmute our end.

"Brava!" Isabelle calls out, applauding. I join in and clap, too.

Lily takes a bow and skips back over to the phone. "Thanks. It's called La Campanella, and it's supposed to imitate the sounds of a bell. It's really fun to play."

"I couldn't believe how fast your fingers were flying," Isabelle says. "I'll have to come hear you in person."

Lily squeals. "I'd love that! When will the snow clear completely?"

Isabelle looks over at me, and I sigh. "I think it will be melted enough for Isabelle to drive down tomorrow."

Isabelle's lips twist to the side, disappointment filling her expression. I know how she feels. I'm not ready for this to be over. We haven't even discussed what's going to happen when we go back to LA.

"You guys should have a party for your last night," Lily says.

"A party?" I ask. "With whom? Lionel?"

"Sure, why not?" Lily says. "He deserves some fun."

I snort a laugh.

"Just eat a fancy dinner… Wait, you probably do that anyway. But wear something extra fancy, dance a little, have some fun. You guys deserve it."

Isabelle and I look at each other, as if trying to gauge whether or not the other person thinks it's ridiculous or genius.

"Let's do it," Isabelle finally says. "I actually think Josephine might be done with my dress."

"You're having Josephine make you a dress?" Lily asks.

"I told her to," I reply.

Lily nods her head in approval. "Smart move, big bro."

I shrug a shoulder, uncomfortable with my little sister's praise.

"Make sure to take pictures," Lily says. "I want to see when you come visit me."

"We will," Isabelle promises.

"Maybe I'll speak with Father about getting you back online." Lily's face lights with delight, so I add quickly, "Within reason."

"Thank you, Adam!" Lily squeals.

The girls say goodbye, and I already feel like Isabelle fits right into my family. Which is further than I expected any of these feelings to go…but how can I deny the way I feel?

"So, party tonight?" Isabelle asks.

"Party tonight," I confirm. I check the time on my phone— two in the afternoon. "I should probably let Lionel know so they can prepare the ballroom."

Isabelle nods and presses a sweet kiss to my lips. "I'll see you at dinner, then."

I feel like a teenage boy again, excited to see the girl I'm interested in at a party that night. While I should be disappointed in myself for such feelings, I can't help enjoying the way she's worked her way into my heart. "See you then."

ISABELLE LEAVES to do a final dress fitting with Josephine, and I take the opportunity to call my father and Henry. It's been a few months since I've spoken to them. I know I've disappointed them both greatly, and I don't have much to say to make things better. But the three of us have agreed to form a task force of sorts to manage Lily, and hopefully the three of us together can keep her safe.

I don't pay attention to the notifications on my phone that have piled up over the last three days, choosing instead to focus on the task at hand. I sit in my office chair, dial my father's number, and look again at the picture of our family in the cracked glass. Guilt washes over me at being unable to protect Lily. She needed someone's guidance. After my mother's death, Father and Henry threw themselves into the business, although they tried their best to split their attention between Stone Technologies and raising Lily through her teenage years. But I completely ignored all of them, except the one fateful night I unwittingly created the circumstances for Lily and Tristan to meet.

It's all my fault, and I'm doing everything in my power to rectify my errors.

"Adam." My father's voice comes through the speakerphone. There's little emotion in his voice, but I didn't expect a warm greeting.

"Hello, Father. I wanted to speak with you and Henry about Lily."

"Thank you, Adam," he says, sarcasm tinging his words. "I'm doing well. How are you?"

I heave a sigh. "How are you, Father?"

"Genuinely, I'm well. And I am glad you're taking an interest in your sister. I'll dial Henry." I hear some beeps on his end, then ringing.

"Hello, Father. Adam." Henry's voice sounds just as impassive as Father's.

"Hello, Henry," I say, attempting a cordial greeting this time. "How are you?"

Silence.

"Are you there?" I ask.

"Yes," Henry says. "I'm recovering from your interest in someone other than yourself."

"Ha ha." If only they could see the scowl on my face. "I wanted to speak with you and Father about Lily. She called earlier and wanted to discuss her Internet restrictions. Have you spoken with her lately?"

"Luna and I visited last weekend," Henry says. "She seems like she's doing much better. And Luna calls her almost daily. She says she's nearly back to herself."

"I have to agree," Father says. "She's showing her personality again. She practices the piano all day, but she doesn't withdraw nearly as much as she did before. I feel very confident in her progress."

"That's how it seemed to me, as well," I say. "So, she's returned to herself, but can we trust her to not make the same mistakes again?"

"That's the question," Father says. "I'm not so sure. She's still so naive and optimistic."

"True," Henry says. "But how will she learn unless she gets some experience?"

"*Experience* is what led us to the situation we're in," Father says sharply. "Sometimes experience is not the teacher we need."

"But she deserves to live!" Henry exclaims, more passionate than usual. "What kind of life does she have in the penthouse?"

"She has everything she needs," Father retorts. "Her protection is of the utmost importance."

"I agree, Father," I cut in. "But I'm not suggesting she has all her typical freedoms. She's just asking about getting Internet access for now. I believe that would be a way to ease her back to normalcy."

Father and Henry are quiet for a minute. Finally, I hear Father say, "Fine. But I need to be able to monitor who she contacts."

"Of course," I say. "Although I doubt she'd be interested in having any contact with...you know."

Father grunts in agreement.

"We do need to discuss her future," Henry says. "She hasn't had a chance to finish her degree. Maybe with Internet access she can at least take some online college classes."

"That's a good point," Father says.

"But she also needs to look forward to leaving the penthouse," Henry continues. "I've spoken to Aunt Agatha and she says she'd be happy to take her in. I believe letting her return to normalcy in Brookhaven would be safer than Silver Lake City."

"Now, Henry–" Father begins.

"He's right," I cut in. "I know you want to protect her, but we have to think about her future. Brookhaven is a small town, it would be perfect for her to begin experiencing normal life again. If we keep her locked up forever, it'll have the opposite effect of our desired goal. Either she'll find a way to rebel, or she'll lose all semblance of reality."

Father is quiet for a moment. "I'll consider it. But for now, just Internet access. And she has to enroll in college classes."

"Agreed," I reply.

"Adam, I have to ask where this is coming from," Henry says. "I thought you wanted to keep her locked down as much as possible."

"I did." My eyes stray to the picture again, my heart clenching with the memory of happier times when we were whole. "But I think it's time to help her heal instead of shielding her from the world." I pause before my next words. "I think it's what Mother would have wanted."

Silence hangs heavy.

"Perhaps you're right," Father finally says.

"And perhaps there's someone who's helping influence your decisions," Henry says, the implication clear in his words.

"And perhaps you can mind your own business," I say sharply.

Henry just laughs. "I look forward to meeting her. If your feelings are what I believe them to be, the snow must be nearly clear by now."

"Yes. We're supposed to come back home tomorrow."

"Then we'll arrange a meeting. I'm sure Luna would love to meet her, as well."

"Thank you for calling, Adam," Father says. "I hope we can have more communication in the future, and not just about Lily."

I swallow hard, a lump in my throat. "I hope so, as well."

With that, the three of us hang up the phone. A glint of light hits the photo in the frame, and again I think I can see out of my left eye. It's faint, but light is now coming through. I sense the lightness in my chest, a result of Isabelle healing all the cracks in my soul, more than she will ever understand.

CHAPTER
Twenty~Nine
ISABELLE

I stand outside the double doors of the ballroom, ready to see Adam. He had Lionel tell me to meet him there instead of in the dining room. It feels so old-fashioned and I absolutely adore it.

Speaking of old-fashioned, my dress is FABULOUS. The fabric is a mix between yellow and gold, and it actually sparkles. It's sleeveless, with a deep V neckline and fitted until just below my waist, then it flows out with the most incredible volume. Somehow Brigette found a pair of gold heels to match that actually fit me. I had her curl my hair in waves, and she did my makeup with dark lashes and red lipstick. I can't wait for Adam to see.

Lionel gives me a little nod and smile. "You look lovely, Ms. Isabelle," he says.

"Thank you, Lionel. Will you be dancing with us?"

He shifts, uncomfortable. "Mr. Stone has requested that I do, but I'm not sure I'll have a partner."

I raise a brow. "I think Josephine wouldn't mind having you lead her in a dance."

From the way his eyes widen, I'm now certain I haven't

misread the signals between them. "Perhaps you're right," he says.

Then he swings the doors open, and I step into the ballroom. The entire gigantic room is lit by candles, the soft glow making the chandelier sparkle in the middle of the high ceiling. The floor is gleaming marble, and the walls are decorated with ornate wood carvings separating the panels of deep blue curtains. I can't imagine a more romantic room in the world.

Standing in the center of the dance floor is Adam. He's wearing a dark blue suit, a light blue shirt, and a white bow tie. Tucked into his front pocket is a red rose. But it's the look in his eyes that takes my breath away. The heat in his gaze threatens to burn me on the spot. Desire. Passion. Longing. Everything I feel is reflected in his expression, and I want nothing more than to be in his arms, having him hold me close.

He holds his hand out to me, and as I approach, he gives a small bow. "May I have this dance?" he asks.

"You may," I reply, a coy smile on my lips. He draws me in, holding one hand in his, and his other arm around my waist, pulling me close.

The first few notes of "Music of the Night" sound through the room, and I stifle a giggle. "Are we embracing the phantom mood tonight?"

"I thought it was appropriate," he replies.

This song has never seemed so romantic, with Adam's arm around my waist, pulling me close to him, and my hand held in his. I breathe him in, his scent reminding me of the woods around us, and I feel like I could stay here forever.

I look around the room, noticing that all the staff are dressed in their finest clothes, but they're not joining us on the dance floor. "Why are they just watching us?" I ask.

"I asked them to let us have this first dance," Adam replies.

"Like a wedding," I say with a smile, then immediately

regret my words. Did I just bring up a wedding with Adam Stone?

But he doesn't seem fazed, and he just grins down at me. "Like a wedding," he confirms.

Be still, my heart.

We sway through the rest of the song, and after it's done, everyone around the room claps. Even Mario lets out a little whistle, and my cheeks flush. Adam just takes me by the hand and leads me to the table set for two in the corner of the ballroom. "Let's eat, and then we can dance some more."

I follow him over to the elaborately decorated table for two, with a satin tablecloth and red roses in the center. He pulls out my chair, like a perfect gentleman, then sits across from me.

"You know, the first night I came here, I wondered if you'd make me sit across the giant dining table from you," I say.

He smirks. "I'm not that cold, am I?"

I shrug a shoulder. "Not anymore."

He pauses, and his face turns serious. "I am sorry for the way I treated you when you first arrived."

"I know." I reach across the table and take his hand. "But you've proven to me that you're not actually cold and harsh."

He swallows hard, his eyes locked on mine. "When you say it, I almost believe it."

I squeeze his hand tight, hoping I can impart the truth in my words. "It's true. Believe it."

His eyes gleam with something that almost looks like love, and before I can overanalyze it, the footmen arrive with our dinner dishes.

"Beef Wellington?!" I squeal. "I didn't know they could make this!"

"I asked Mario and we made it happen," Adam says. "I hope you like it."

The smell fills my senses, and I'm embarrassed that I almost cry from the familiarity. I take my first bite, nearly burning my mouth in the process, but it's worth it for the taste. "This is incredible. Even better than I remembered."

"I'm so glad," Adam says. He's been watching me and hasn't taken a bite yet, but now he picks up his fork and digs in, too.

We eat in silence for the next few minutes, but it's completely different from those nights where Adam gave me the silent treatment. We catch each other's eyes and smile, a comfortable silence where we know we don't have to say anything, but we can if we want.

Dessert is served, and it's a butter cake with whipped cream. I could lick the whole plate and almost do. When I finally look up at Adam, his eyes are twinkling with amusement.

"What?" I ask.

He motions at the side of his mouth. "You have a little cream left there."

I wipe my mouth with the napkin, but he shakes his head and laughs. He stands from his chair and steps around the table to me. "Let me," he says, and bends down, kissing the side of my mouth.

Shivers run down my spine. We've shared many kisses this week, more than I can count, but each time his lips meet mine feels like the first. I can't get enough. He moves from the side of my mouth to give me a proper kiss, his lips melting into mine as he leans over my chair.

I pull back, a little embarrassed at our public display.

"What's wrong?" Adam asks.

I gesture at the people around us. "We haven't really...you know, kissed that much in front of everyone." I lean in and whisper, "Like Lionel."

Adam glances over his shoulder at his trusted friend, who just smiles and gives him a thumbs up. "I don't think he minds," he says, then wraps his arm around my waist and pulls me to standing, flush against his body.

I let out a little gasp of surprise. Adam groans low and kisses me again, deeply this time, and I let myself forget about everyone around us. His hands grasp my waist, a sense of urgency in his kisses and his hold, as if he knows that this bubble around us is going to burst when we leave here tomorrow.

Tomorrow.

I pull back again, and peer into his eyes. The eyes I've come to know and admire. One crystal blue, one faded and hazy. And in those eyes are the two sides of Adam that I know—on the one hand, generous and protective; but on the other hand, gruff and stern. They're two halves that make up a whole person, the person I want by my side each day.

"What happens tomorrow?" I ask softly.

Adam tilts his head. "Tomorrow?" he repeats, his voice raspy.

"When we leave."

"Oh." His hands settle heavy on my hips, our bodies still close together. "We go back to LA. And we make the movie together."

I nod once, already knowing that piece of our future. "And when we're not making the movie?" I ask slowly.

"And when we're not making the movie..." He dips his head, presses his lips against mine, and says, "We'll be doing a lot more of this."

I let out a breath, relief flooding my body. "I was worried this was just...you know..."

"Stockholm Syndrome?" Adam supplies.

I laugh out loud, tipping my head back. "That's not what I would call it."

"Of course it's not. You're the prisoner in the scenario."

"Well, either way, I wanted to make sure this wasn't just a fling by forced proximity."

His expression softens, and he holds my gaze. "This isn't a fling. And, yes, forced proximity brought us together and helped me realize what a jerk I've been. But what's happening here between us..." He swallows hard. "It feels a lot like—"

"Mr. Stone!" Lionel's voice rings across the ballroom. He has a phone up to his ear, and he looks desperate.

"What is it, Lionel?" Adam asks.

Lionel crosses the ballroom to us, his steps quick and light. "You've received an urgent phone call." He holds the phone out to us.

We both look at the screen. I'm sure Adam worries that it's Lily, because that's what I'm assuming.

But it's not. It's my father.

CHAPTER
Thirty

ADAM

I put the call on speakerphone and hold the phone between us so Isabelle can hear, as well. "Jim? What's wrong?"

"I've been calling you for three days," he says, anger dripping from his words. "Why have neither of you picked up?"

I look at Isabelle, whose guilty expression likely mimics mine. "We've been...busy," I finally say.

"Whatever you've been doing isn't as important as this. Tristan Jackson has been running a smear campaign against you. And now the production company wants to pull you from the movie."

"Wait, which one of us?" Isabelle asks.

"Adam," Jim replies.

My stomach sinks. I shouldn't be surprised, but in truth, I didn't think there was a possibility of me losing this role. Jim swore he had the production company's confirmation.

Isabelle's eyes turn wide as she meets my gaze. "What is Tristan saying?"

"Isn't it obvious?" I say sharply. "That I'm unfit to act for a family-friendly network with my reputation."

Isabelle's expression turns to fury. "Dad? Is that true?"

We hear him huff a sigh through the speaker. "Yes. That's exactly what he's saying. Along with the mystery of Adam's scar. Adam, you know I can't spin that one in a positive way."

"I'm aware," I mutter.

"And without any information about why you punched him, I can't spin that either," Jim continues.

"Adam," Isabelle says softly, her eyes on mine. "You have to come forward. What he's doing now is a direct attack on you."

I shake my head. "It's in the contract. I can't."

"Isn't this slander? Defamation of character?" Isabelle asks her dad.

"He's not saying anything that isn't true," Jim answers. "He's calling out your reputation, making himself look like a victim for being attacked at the Goldies, and saying that you've got the scars now to prove your bad reputation. Unfortunately, he caught the ear of the production company, and they want him instead."

I clench my jaw. "So not only are they pulling me, but they want *him* instead?"

"That's what it looks like," Jim answers.

Anger boils within me. This man has cost me my savings, ruined my sister's life, and now he's directly coming for me. Taking EVERY good thing that has ever happened to me—and now, that includes Isabelle.

And there's nothing I can do about it.

I let out a frustrated sound, something like a growl, and hand Isabelle the phone. I start pacing around the ballroom; I can't take part in this conversation anymore.

"Isabelle, you need to come home," Jim says. "We need to at least show that you're ready to do the movie."

"I'm not doing it without Adam," she says.

I turn back to Isabelle. "Yes, you are."

"No, I'm not." She doesn't back down from my glare. "Not after what you've told me about Tristan."

"What do you know about Tristan?" Jim interjects.

"Nothing!" I bark. "She knows nothing." I narrow my eyes at her. "You swore you wouldn't tell."

She shakes her head. "I know. But this is going too far."

"No!" I pace away from her, running a hand through my hair. "You will not ruin your own career and reputation for the sake of mine." I walk back to her and grab the phone. "Jim, Isabelle will see you tomorrow. Thank you for the call." I hang up before he can say anything else and hand the phone to Lionel. Taking her hands in mine, I look down at her. I take a steadying breath and soften my voice. "You are going to take the role. You will act with Tristan, and you'll have your first big break."

Her eyes are wet with unshed tears. She shakes her head. "No. I won't do it. I can't."

"You can," I insist. "You're an incredible actress. I know you can do it. And it will all be worth it in the end."

"But what about you?" she presses. "This movie was supposed to be your return to acting. You need this role."

She's right. I know she is. But I can't let her see how desperate I was to act again. "I'll be fine."

"No. We're going to fight this. We'll make sure everyone knows that Tristan is wrong."

"He's not wrong!" I cry out, stepping back from her. I gesture at my face. "You don't even know what happened when I got this scar."

She gives her head a tiny shake.

"I was drunk, Isabelle." I laugh. "I was drunk, depressed out of my mind, and miserable that Tristan had ruined Lily. And I decided to drive my car down the mountain to see her." I gesture out toward the window. "You know how treacherous the drive is. Only an idiot would attempt to do it while intoxicated."

"So you made a mistake," Isabelle says. "We all do. But I think it's pretty clear that you've learned to do better."

"Is it?" I shake my head. "That's who I am, can't you see? I'm still that same man. I'm selfish and arrogant and—"

"No, you're not." Isabelle takes my hands in hers. Her soft touch is enough to calm me down. "Someone who's truly selfish and arrogant wouldn't say those words about themselves. You're a little rough around the edges, but we all are in our own ways." She rests her gentle hands on my face, and I close my eyes, allowing myself a moment to revel in her touch on my cheeks. "You're protective. Caring. A little aggressive and arrogant—"

I snort a laugh, despite myself.

"But that's just the exterior. In here," she places one hand on my heart, "is a generous man who will do anything to keep his loved ones safe."

She reaches up and kisses me softly. When she says these things, I can almost believe her words.

Almost.

She pulls back. "You can fight this, Adam. We can fight this together."

I shake my head at her. "I've lost the fight, Isabelle. I'm past redemption. But you're not." I hold her tightly around the waist with one arm, using my other hand to cradle her cheek. "You don't need to drag yourself down with me. I've ruined my chance for the future, but I want you to go. Leave me and this place, and be happy."

Her eyes glisten with tears. "I don't want to act with Tristan," she says. "I wanted to do the movie with you."

Each word she says pierces into my heart. How far we've

come from our first meeting, and how far we're about to fall. But I put on a brave face, like the actor I am.

"Trust me, that's what I wanted, too. But you can manage. In your career, you'll have to act with plenty of people you don't like. It'll be good practice." I lift the side of my mouth, the best attempt I can make at a smile. "I can't wait to see how you do."

"Won't you come with me?" she pleads.

I shake my head, stroking her cheek with my thumb. "I'm done. There's nothing left for me in LA. I'll just stay here at the castle until I get my things in order, and then...I'll have to figure out my plan for the future."

"Maybe your brother will help you out," she offers.

"Probably." I don't tell her that the idea of returning home with my tail between my legs makes me want to cringe. But maybe that's part of the redemption I need. "You should go to bed."

"I don't want to," she whispers. "Let's just spend the night watching movies together. Our last few hours in a bubble."

Her offer tugs at my heart, but I can't. I need to sever the ties between us sooner rather than later.

I want to be with Isabelle. I've fallen for her—no, I'm in love with her. And I've never truly been in love before. But loving someone means sacrificing your own happiness for theirs. Isabelle will never be happy if she loses herself to protect me.

Life with her in the castle has been almost perfect. As much as I want to keep up this paradise, she deserves more. Isabelle deserves her time in the spotlight. She deserves the attention and praise that will come her way, as soon as she gets her opportunity to shine.

So I shake my head again. "I don't want to keep you awake when you have to drive down the mountain tomorrow." I kiss her forehead, lingering there and taking one last inhale of her soft skin. This is goodbye.

When I pull away, two tears are tracing down her cheeks. She opens her eyes, her wet lashes shining in the candlelight, and she has fire in her eyes. "I won't give up, Adam." She grabs me tightly, burying her head in my chest.

If I don't leave now, I never will. I remove myself from her grasp and turn around before she can convince me to stay. My heart feels like it's been ripped in two. First Tristan takes Lily, and now he takes Isabelle. But perhaps it's what I deserve after everything I've done, selfishly ignoring my family for years. Who am I to think I deserve someone as kind, gentle, and compassionate as Isabelle?

She deserves more than me.

Thirty~One

ISABELLE

I didn't sleep a wink. And, no, it's not because I couldn't watch any movies.

It's because I've been plotting. Or at least *trying* to plot.

Adam might think we're done. He might not want to fight Tristan, but I do. Men like Tristan do not deserve to win, and I'm going to make sure of it. But I can't come up with any kind of plan, and it's killing me. I can see why Adam feels so hopeless.

It's eight in the morning, and I'm all packed and ready to leave. I'm wearing the same outfit I wore my first night here—my black slacks, deep purple tank top, and stilettos. But I feel like a completely different person, like I've lived an entire lifetime here at the castle instead of just a couple weeks. After saying goodbye to everyone in the kitchen, I make my way to the front entrance, waiting to see Adam one more time. My stomach is in knots. Just the thought of leaving him makes me sick. But I have to hope I can somehow help fix this mess he's in.

"Is everything ready?" Lionel asks, picking up my bag. I

packed the gold dress and the bunny slippers, knowing that Adam would want me to have them.

"Uh, yes. I just thought Adam would be here."

"Unfortunately, he's been detained," Lionel says.

"Oh."

My heart sinks. Maybe I don't mean as much to him as he does to me. But I can't believe that. Not after the way he held and kissed me last night. It really felt like one of those "if you love them, let them go" kind of moments.

"Isabelle!" Theo's voice echoes through the hallway, followed by the sound of his little feet pattering toward me. He wraps me in a huge hug around my thighs. "Don't leave without saying goodbye!"

"Of course not," I reply, rubbing his head. I kneel down in front of him. "Are you going home soon, too?"

He nods. "Daddy is supposed to come get me tomorrow."

"That's great. I bet you're excited to go home."

He shrugs. "I wanted to build another Snow Hulk. Maybe in the winter you can come back and we can build one again!"

"That sounds great," I say.

"Theo!" Brigette rushes over to us. "Becca couldn't find you again, you silly boy. Don't frighten her."

Theo smirks at me, an expression far too old for his age, and I laugh.

Brigette wraps me in one of her cushioned hugs. "Goodbye, Isabelle." She pulls back and looks me in the eye. I can tell she's searching my expression and finds something she approves of. A small smile fills her face. "But this isn't really goodbye, is it?"

I lean in toward her. "Not if I can help it," I whisper.

Her eyes twinkle. "I hope you're right." She squeezes my shoulders, and the pang in my chest intensifies. I'm going to miss Adam more than I would have ever expected. But Brigette, Lionel, Theo, Josephine, Mario...they've all become family, too.

I nod at Lionel, who picks up my suitcase, and we head outside to my car. The sun is shining, and it's warm outside. It's hard to believe this whole area was covered in snow just a few days ago.

"Oh, Philippe," I say, running a hand over the hood.

Lionel tries to hide a smile as he opens the trunk and sets my bags inside. "I trust you'll be able to find your way back down."

I nod. "There isn't really any way to go but down from here."

He closes the trunk and gives me a little bow. "It's been an honor serving you. I do hope to see you again."

I take a step toward him and envelop him in a big hug. His hugs aren't nearly as cushioned as Brigette's, but there's still a familiar, homey feel to him. "Thank you, Lionel." I pull away and smile at him. "I'll see you again soon. I promise."

"I look forward to it." He steps to the driver's door and opens it, and I climb inside. I glance back up at the castle, and I swear I can see a flutter of the curtain upstairs. Was that Adam? Is he watching me leave?

I start the car, the sensation of the engine rumbling almost foreign after the amount of time I've spent in the castle. I can't believe I'm actually leaving. Half of me feels like this experience has been a dream, and the other half feels like this castle is where I'm meant to be. But there's no time to dwell on these thoughts. Because if I'm going to help Adam, I need to leave. I shift the car into drive and start heading down the mountain.

As I drive, it begins to rain.

I was sure Lionel and Agatha were joking about the weather reflecting the mood of the resident, but I can't help wondering if the rain is a sign of Adam's temperament.

I think about the way he was when I first came here. Just like a snowstorm, quietly furious. Cold and intense, holding everything inside and not letting me see the light. I laugh to myself, remembering the days when he gave me the silent treatment and I kept saying ridiculous things to make him break. Even then, I knew that there had to be deep feelings hidden underneath the surface.

It wasn't until he saved me in the forest that I really suspected how deep those feelings went. When I realized how much he cared for and loved Lily, and then his mother, it all came together.

Thinking of Lily renews my determination to see this plan through. I won't break any promises to Adam; I want to deserve his trust. But I don't know how I'll be able to manage it.

As I drive down the mountain, tightly gripping the steering wheel, racking my brain for some semblance of a plan, my phone rings. It's a call from an unknown number, the area code showing it's someone from LA. A casting director? It's always worth it to pick up an unknown number, even with the risk of it being a telemarketer.

I press the button to answer the call from my Bluetooth speaker. "Hello?"

"Hello, is this Isabelle Lovett?" A cheerful, male voice rings through my car.

"It is. Who is this?"

A small chuckle sounds through the speaker. "I apologize for calling unannounced. But I figured I should introduce myself, since we'll be working together." A pause. "My name is Tristan Jackson."

I recoil in shock, my arms jerking the steering wheel to the left. I let out a squeal of terror, but thankfully no one is coming the other direction. I tilt the wheel to the right and get back on my side of the road.

"Hello? Are you all right?"

"Yes, hello. I'm here. I'm just...driving." I can't help the coldness that comes through my voice. I'm finally talking to TRISTAN JACKSON, aka the worst human being alive, as far as I'm concerned.

"Ah, I'm sorry for distracting you. Is this a bad time?"

I want to say yes, but I also want to know what exactly he's trying to pull here. "No, it's fine. I can talk while I drive."

"Great. Well, like I said, I wanted to introduce myself to you. I read about your interview, and I was so impressed. I'm so sorry Adam showed you up like that. He tends to steal the spotlight at the most inconvenient moments."

I stay silent. Is this the way he views things? That Adam stole the spotlight from him when he first started acting? And that he continues to do that in their careers?

He clears his throat. "Anyway, I was so intrigued by you that I asked around and finally got your phone number. I wanted to see if you'd be interested in having dinner together. Maybe some drinks. We could go dancing." I swear I can hear his smile through the phone. "I haven't met anyone like you in the industry. I can tell there's something special about you, and I think we should get to know each other before we start the movie in a few weeks."

Oh, wow.

This guy is good.

Truth be told, if I didn't know anything that Adam had told me, I would have been flattered. That little shiver of "he likes me!" would have rushed down my spine, the tingle that tells you that you're special, and this guy has picked you out of everyone else for his attention.

For a moment, I hesitate. Who do I believe? Is Adam telling the truth about Tristan?

Yes. I trust Adam.

Adam has shared everything with me. At this point, I feel like our souls are connected. And even besides that, I've seen Lily and spoken with her.

This pathetic excuse for a man took everything from her, and I won't let it happen again.

"I'll have to pass," I say. "But thank you for the offer."

He doesn't say anything for a moment, and then he laughs, still light-hearted. "What do you mean?"

"I mean exactly what I said. I'll pass on spending any kind of time with you."

"May I ask why?" His voice is sharper now, with a bit of an edge.

I pause. I have to be careful what I say to him, to avoid Adam getting into trouble for telling me the truth. I never found out if the contract meant he couldn't speak about the incident publicly or if he wasn't supposed to say anything at all.

"I'm doing the movie with Adam," I finally say. "I'm not sure where you got the idea that you would be in it instead of him."

"Adam Stone—" His name comes out like a growl, but Tristan stops himself and clears his throat, back to his cheerful tone. "Adam Stone is no longer their choice."

"Not if I have anything to say about it," I reply.

There's silence for a couple of moments, and then he speaks again, his voice low and menacing. "Listen here. Adam Stone deserves nothing in this industry. Nothing! I've worked for everything I have, and no one can take that away from me." He pauses. "Watch your back, Isabelle. You don't want to get on my bad side."

And then he hangs up.

My hands are shaking, my heart is racing, and I have to suppress the urge to shiver. Yeah, that was creepy. And not just the threat. I'm willing to take my chances with him. But the clear switch, the way he acted so sweet and charming and suddenly flipped it on its head—terrifying.

Poor Lily.

I can absolutely see how a woman would fall for his charms. How many women has he already done this to? There's no way Lily was the first.

And there it is. My plan to save Adam is finally clear.

I take a steadying breath and dial Jen's number on my phone.

"Isabelle?" Jen's voice sounds through my speakers. "Where have you been? I haven't heard from you in days!"

"Hey, girl. Yeah, I'm driving down the mountain now."

"Everyone is buzzing about Adam and Tristan. You guys unleashed so much drama. Is Adam coming down, too?"

"No. He's staying up at the castle. He's...giving up."

"Seriously? That doesn't sound like Adam Stone."

I huff a laugh. "You'd think so. But I think he's tired of fighting. Tristan has hit him from every angle, and he doesn't want to try anymore." I straighten in my seat. "But I'm not giving up. I want to take Tristan down."

"Seriously? *You* want to take Tristan Jackson down?" Jen laughs. "And how exactly do you plan to do that?"

"With your help."

"What...what do you mean?"

I wish I could tell her everything. But I promised Adam I wouldn't. "I need you to use your super tech skills to find a list of girls that Tristan has had contact with in the last five years. A lot of them might not be public. But if anyone can find out, you can."

"Do I have your permission to use my illegal skills?"

"I'm going to pretend you didn't say that."

She pauses. "Wait. You're serious about this?"

"Trust me, Jen. This is bigger than Adam and Tristan. If I

have any idea what's going on, we're about to uncover a huge scandal with Tristan Jackson at the center. And in the process, we're going to help a lot of women, too."

Jen pauses, taking in my words, and I hope beyond hope that she will agree to help.

"Well, in that case, I'm in."

Thirty-Two

ADAM

The castle feels so empty without Isabelle. My days are long and boring. I spend most of my time in the theater, watching the movies we watched together, trying to gather my courage to call my brother Henry and ask for his help. I could hide out here in the castle for a while longer, but at some point, I need to live.

My phone rings with a call from Aunt Agatha. I snort as I pick it up. "Hello, Aunt."

"Adam, my dear, what a mess you've made."

If there's one thing I don't need, it's my aunt rubbing my failures in my face. "Thank you for instilling your confidence."

"Oh, hush, you cheeky boy."

I chuckle. "Why exactly did you call? Just to chastise me?"

"Of course not. I want to know if you're going to face your fears or let them rule you."

I lay back on the sofa, my hand covering my eyes. "I don't know what you mean."

"Yes, you do. You're probably lounging somewhere in the castle, whining about your disappointing life and how much you wish you could just ignore the real life going on around you.

Well, let me tell you something. No matter how hard you try, you're going to have to face reality at some point. And that includes that idiot, Trevor Johnson."

"You mean Tristan Jackson."

"I don't care. He's an idiot and does not deserve a space in my memory bank. I'm getting old, my dear, and I'm selective about what or who earns a spot in my mind. And that boy does not earn anything from me. Not after what he did to Lily and what he's doing to you, too."

"I appreciate your confidence in me, Aunt, but he's right."

She titters a high-pitched laugh. "He's RIGHT? About you? Nonsense."

"It's true," I insist. "I'm selfish, hot-headed—"

"Now, is that what that beautiful brunette would say about you?"

"I—" I swallow hard. "I don't know."

"Oh, I do. She would say that you're wrong. In fact, she *has* said that to you, hasn't she?"

My silence is enough of an answer for her.

"You can't hide anymore. Enough is enough. Be a man and face the situation. Take Trevor down."

I snort a laugh. "I'll think about it." But I won't. I already know that I'm done trying.

"All right. Now that I've said my piece, I'll tell you about my book club." She prattles on for another ten minutes about her latest read, a pirate romance, which explains the eyepatch she wore last week.

We hang up, and I can't bring myself to sit and watch the movie anymore. I rest back in my chair, staring up at the ceiling.

My phone buzzes with a text message. It's from an unknown number. I open the message and my stomach sinks.

There's no question who that is. With a panic, I dial Lily's number. Has he already gotten to her? Is she all right?

The video call rings a few times, and then she picks up, her smile lighting my whole screen. I can finally breathe. "Hey Adam! What's up?"

"Are you all right?" The words rush out of my mouth.

She furrows her brow. "I'm fine."

"You haven't been contacted by Tristan?"

Her head rears back. "No. Of course not. I don't even have access to anyone besides family. Dad finally gave me some limited Internet access, so I got to see everyone lose their minds over seeing you again." She tilts her head. "Is everything okay?"

Do I tell her about the text? No. I don't want to worry her. "Everything's fine. I shouldn't have called."

"No," she says quickly. "I'm glad you did." She brushes a piece of her long, blonde hair over her shoulder. "You need a plan."

"A plan?" I scoff. "My plan is to find a new career."

"You can't hide forever! And you can't let him win!"

"You sound like Agatha," I mutter.

"I'm serious, Adam." She bites a nail for a moment, and I can tell she's contemplating her next words. I give her the time she needs to gather her thoughts.

"I'm angry, Adam." she says, her cheeks turning pink. "I know you still see me as the little girl who got lost in the woods, and yes, I made some mistakes last year. But I'm not heartbroken anymore. In fact, I'm not broken at all. I'm ANGRY. And Tristan doesn't deserve to get away with this."

She's right about that. He doesn't. But it's not worth the danger of what he could do to her again.

"You need to say something," Lily continues. "You can tell everyone what happened with me, and—"

"No." I need to shut that line of thought down before she gets too far. "I would never compromise you like that. Besides, it's in the contract."

Her brows furrow. "But this is defamation of character. Surely you can breach the contract."

"I refuse to risk it. You don't need that kind of stress, anyway. If any word came out about your relationship with Tristan, the paparazzi would be all over you. Tristan would…" I cut myself off before saying that he would somehow try to get back at her. "You wouldn't be able to leave your home."

"I already don't leave," she says, anger lacing her words. "I'm not allowed to. Because you all think I'm a child."

"That's not…I don't think you're a child," I say gently. "Father just wants to make sure you don't have another situation like you did with Tristan."

"And keeping me locked up is the solution?"

"No, of course not." This conversation is going off the rails, and I need to get it back on track. "Look, I'll talk to Father again. You're right. It's been long enough that you've been cooped up there, and it's not like you're doing anything reckless."

"And you'll find some way to get back at Tristan?"

"I'll think about it." Sure, I'll get back at him, if hiding out here in the castle counts. I don't want to end our conversation this way, though. "How has piano practice been?"

"Good. I'm working on a few Debussy pieces now."

"I thought you already played those?"

She nods. "I've been playing Clair de Lune for years. But I never attempted Reverie. It's not too difficult, but it's so dreamy." She raises her brows at me. "Maybe if you convince Father to let me out of here, I can finally perform again."

"Don't push it," I say teasingly. "Why don't you perform for me right now?"

"Okay!" She hops up and sets her phone down on the fireplace mantle, positioning it so I can see her at the grand piano. I remember when she was four years old and learning to play on that same exact piano, her feet dangling from the bench as she played and sang a little song about a robot.

But she's not that little four-year-old anymore. Her blonde hair has grown with her, and her arms and legs have lengthened but don't look as knobby as before. She sits at the piano, gracefully brushing her hair behind her shoulders, and she inhales as she sets her fingers on the keys. Her left hand plays a few notes, and as the right hand joins in, it truly does sound like a dream.

My heart twists as I listen and watch her. She has a special gift, healing others with the power of music. It's a gift that deserves to be shared with the world, and it was supposed to be, before Tristan took that away from her.

The music is supposed to feel like a dream, relaxing me, but instead, I feel angry. Angry at Tristan for what he stole from Lily —her guaranteed future as a concert pianist.

Her freedom to fall in love.

Her innocence.

Her love of life.

And then I think about what he's taken from me:

My career.

My confidence as a man.

And, worst of all, my relationship with Isabelle.

But I'm so tired. I'm so tired of fighting Tristan and losing. I don't know if I can find the strength to try again, especially if it means that he'll come after Lily. I failed to keep her safe once, and I'll never make that mistake again.

Thirty-Three

ISABELLE

A week after I leave the castle, I now have the evidence I need to take Tristan down.

Maybe.

Just as I anticipated, Lily wasn't the first woman Tristan manipulated and tossed aside. He has a long list of women, at least a dozen, who fell for his charms and realized he wasn't truly in love with *them*, but what they could give him.

Seven of them are willing to come forward. Two of them want to remain anonymous, but the other five are ready to put everything on the line for the sake of protecting other women.

The problem is that people don't always believe women who come forward about their manipulators. Sometimes it even backfires and the women get made to look like they're trying to get attention, and the man in question gains popularity. I just hope that isn't what happens here. At the bare minimum, I hope that the Family Entertainment Network won't want to associate themselves with Tristan when his reputation is in question.

I flop back on my couch, having finished my last phone call

with the fifth woman who wants to tell her story. Tomorrow morning we'll contact Allegra at Inside Scoop, the same company who published my interview, and hope they'll run the story.

Jen is still working in her office, tying up all the loose ends. I close my eyes and try to relax, but I don't think I'll be able to until everything is out in the open.

I haven't even tried contacting Adam yet. But he hasn't tried to call me either. Once everything is exposed, I'll call him. Right now, I wouldn't know what to say. I can't let him know what I'm planning, but I also don't want to lie to him.

I hear Jen step into the living room and open my eyes. She leans against the doorframe, her arms crossed in front of her chest. "You kept something from me," she says.

I sit up. "What do you mean?"

"There's one more woman for our list." She stares me down. "Lily Stone."

"How…" I swallow. I didn't think she'd be able to find her connection to Tristan now that she's been locked down. "How did you figure it out?"

She fixes me with a no-nonsense glare. "Really? You didn't think with my 'super tech skills' that I'd be able to put that together? Adam punches Tristan, Lily goes incognito, and now you're on a rampage to find these women who Tristan manipulated. It's pretty clear."

"When you put it that way…" I run a hand through my hair, calculating my words so I don't break my promises to Adam.

But Jen makes it easy for me and starts talking. "Here's what I think happened: Tristan manipulated Lily into falling for him, said something to Adam about it at the Goldies, and Adam punched him. Somehow Adam got to Tristan and convinced him to let Lily go, and Tristan dropped the charges in exchange for them not saying anything." She smirks at me. "How was that?"

"Pretty impressive," I admit.

"If we can get Lily to talk—" Jen begins.

I shake my head. "She can't. It's in the contract."

Jen sighs. "Well, I just called and left her a message."

"Jen!" I jump off the couch. "Adam will kill me if she says anything. It's not just the contract. He doesn't want her to face the public backlash."

"She doesn't have to say anything. We might have enough evidence without her. But her story is the most compelling, and it clears Adam's name. You know I'm right."

She is. We both know it. But that's a line I'm not willing to cross.

Jen looks down at her phone. "She's calling me back." She answers the phone and puts it on speaker. "Hi, Lily. I'm here with Isabelle."

"Oh, hi. Hey, Isabelle."

"Hey, Lily," I say gently.

"Thanks for calling me back," Jen says. "So, I'm not sure if you'd be interested in helping out, but I think it would really help Adam's case."

"I just told Jen about the contract," I say. "She didn't know that you weren't legally allowed to say anything before she called."

Lily is quiet. "I never signed the contract."

It takes a minute for her words to sink in. "Wait...what?"

"I never signed." Her words start rushing out. "The negotiations were rushed, and I was never included in the conversation. I was sent a copy after both Tristan and Adam signed, and there wasn't even a line for my signature. But I wasn't planning on saying anything anyway, so it's not like it mattered."

"And you still don't have to," I say. Jen narrows her eyes at me, but I continue. "It would cause a huge tidal wave, and I don't want to pressure you into anything you're not comfortable with."

Jen sighs. "Agreed. It's your decision entirely."

Lily is silent for a long time, and I wonder if she hung up. "I'll think about it," she finally says.

"Thank you for even considering it," I say. "Hopefully the few women we have who agreed to speak up will be enough."

"I hope so," Lily says. "It's good to hear from you, Isabelle."

"You, too. I'll have to come meet you in person one of these days."

"Hopefully with Adam," she responds, a teasing lilt to her voice.

I chuckle. "Yeah, I hope so, too."

THE NEXT DAY, Jen and I sit in front of her laptop at the kitchen table, anxiously awaiting the article. Allegra said it would be published this afternoon. I've been a ball of nerves all morning, hoping that they write something that makes Tristan seem like the pig he is.

Robby, Jen's boyfriend, came over too. He's sitting on the couch playing video games, oblivious to our nerves. Jen explained the situation to him, and while he's sympathetic, I think he prefers his fictional world to our real one.

I refresh the website again. "It's up!"

At the top of the page is an article with the title:

ALLEGATIONS AGAINST TRISTAN JACKSON SURFACE FROM MULTIPLE WOMEN.

I click the article, and Jen and I lean forward to read. The article is pretty straightforward, reporting that Tristan Jackson has been keeping multiple girlfriends at the same time, misleading them into falling for him and then dumping them when he's achieved whatever goal he had in mind.

By the end, it's made clear that he didn't do anything illegal, just...a little sketchy.

I turn to Jen. "Do you think this is enough?"

She winces and shrugs a shoulder. "I'm not sure."

Robby walks by us, sipping on an iced tea. His game must be over. "What's going on?"

"The article just got published," Jen replies.

Robby stands over her shoulder, scanning the article. "Honestly, I don't know if this will make him actually look BAD."

"What do you mean?" I reply.

"There have been a few stories exposing guys who act like this. Dating multiple women at the same time, manipulating them into thinking they're 'the one,' and if anything, it just makes him more desirable. Guys admire their skills, and girls want to be their next conquest."

"Ugh." I sit back in my chair in disgust. "What's wrong with this world?"

"I'm not condoning it," Robby says quickly, straightening and putting up his hands. A little bit of tea sloshes on the floor. "I'm not one of those guys."

"Don't worry, we know," Jen says, a small smirk on her face. Of every guy I've ever met, Robby is probably the furthest from a ladies' man. He's our lovable nerd.

"So, now what?" I ask.

Jen shrugs and looks sympathetic. "We wait, I guess."

We sit and stare at the computer screen. I'm not sure what we're expecting to materialize, but nothing happens. I should probably do an Internet search of Tristan Jackson's name to see if there are any opinion articles written in response, but my phone buzzes on the table, startling us all.

"It's a text from my dad," I say, furrowing a brow. I spoke to him once when I got down the mountain, letting him know I'd be ready to start shooting soon but didn't say anything else about my plans. It was better to leave him in the dark. I unlock the screen and see the following words:

DAD

My house. Now.

Thirty~Four

ISABELLE

I walk up the steps of my childhood home, preparing myself for whatever my dad has in store. My guess is that he's upset with me for trying to meddle in PR affairs—surprise, surprise—which is why I didn't tell him in the first place. But here we are.

The front door has a keypad, and I enter the code and walk right in. "Hey, Dad, I'm here," I call out. I glance around, noting how nothing has changed since I was last here a few months ago. That's to be expected. Our home was always more functional than cute or "homey," lacking the femininity that my mom would have brought. I have to give my dad credit; our clothes were always clean, and we always had food on the table for dinner. Usually takeout. But he did his very best to raise us three girls alone.

"I'm in the kitchen," he calls back.

I wander through the hall until I find him sitting at the kitchen table with a pot of coffee and two mugs. His hair is askew, and his clothes are rumpled. I see my tired dad and my manager all in one, both sides of him battling for their roles in my life. "Sit," he commands.

I do as instructed. "I'm guessing you saw the article," I say.

He nods, looking down at his cup. "Why did you do it?"

I inhale, wondering if I should take the responsibility or go with ignorance.

But he's my dad. So I tell him the truth, not denying my role in it. "Because Adam doesn't deserve what Tristan is doing to him."

When his eyes meet mine, they're not angry. They have a tenderness and softness I haven't seen in years. "You love him."

A little gasp emerges from me. I cover it with a cough and pour some coffee into my mug. "Uh, I don't think I'd say that."

Dad chuckles. "It's okay. You don't have to tell your dad. But you do." He sips his coffee and sets it on the table. "I can't say I didn't see this coming."

I'm careful not to admit to anything. "What do you mean?"

"I've known Adam for a very long time. He's...well, *you* know. You just spent weeks alone with him. But there's been something missing, a lightness. Someone to understand him and his struggles. And I've wondered in the past if that person was you."

"I'm surprised you even considered that."

Dad nods. "I know I don't come across as the most...sentimental type of guy. After your mom died, I realized how much easier it is to be alone. To focus on my career, to raise you girls and send you off in the right directions. But..." He trails off, his gaze down on his coffee. "Man, do I miss your mom."

My eyes widen at this sudden expression, but I let him continue.

"Love is hard, Isabelle. It's sacrifice and compromise. You're two people raised in completely different ways, coming together to make a family. But when you find that person who wants to work hard with you, it doesn't feel like work. It feels like a partnership. It feels like you get to spend every day with your best friend, and the sacrifices don't feel like sacrifices because you *want* to make them happy."

"And that's what you had with Mom?"

He's still for a moment, then he meets my gaze. "Yes. That's what I had with your mom."

"I wish you would have talked about her more."

He puts his hand on mine and squeezes it. "I should have. She was an incredible woman."

I hesitate a moment, then decide if he's being vulnerable, this is my chance to ask him. "I found some baby pictures in the garage. Did she...call me Belle?"

At that, his eyes well with tears. "She did."

My heart warms, even though I had already figured it out. But hearing it confirmed from my dad makes it feel real. My mom was a real person. She loved me, and even though she's gone, I can still carry this piece of her with me.

With Adam.

Dad suddenly pulls his hand back. He's done with reminiscing, but that's okay. This has been more than I ever expected from him. "So. Adam. And you."

I press my lips together. "And...you're okay with that? Even though you know who he is?"

He chuckles. "I know Adam's reputation, but I also know *Adam*. There has been a lot of hurt. He's been wronged many times in the past...and in the present. But if he has someone by his side to support him, I think he'll come out okay."

"If he doesn't get this movie though..."

Dad grimaces. "This might be the end of his career. I'm not sure where he'd go from here."

I nod. "That's what he's worried about."

Dad's phone buzzes on the counter, interrupting our conversation. "Sorry, I have to check if it's someone for work."

I wave him off. "I know." I've known my entire life that

Dad's work came first. It's what makes this conversation so extraordinary.

Dad gets up and checks his phone at the kitchen counter. I take a sip of my coffee, patiently waiting, and then he groans. "Oh, no."

"What is it?"

"Tristan just released a statement."

"What?" I stand and join him at the counter, and Dad clicks on a video link.

"Hello, everyone." The voice and image of Tristan Jackson, Golden Boy of Hollywood, sitting on his couch appears on Dad's screen. My skin crawls at the sound of his voice, especially now that I've talked to him personally. He looks perfect: his blond hair is styled to perfection, his baby-blue eyes shine at the camera, and his tanned skin and white teeth make him look like he's about to be in a toothpaste commercial. "I've unfortunately seen the allegations against me and wanted to take a minute to address them." He pauses and shakes his head. "I'm so ashamed. Not because they're true, but because of the way I have unintentionally misled these women." He leans toward the camera, his expression so genuine. "You see, I've always tried to befriend those in need. I have a soft spot in my heart for those who are not as well-off as myself." He sits back and shrugs, self-deprecating. "I thought my intentions were clear to these women, but I've only desired to make their lives better. If my actions were misconstrued as romantic, I sincerely apologize. It pains me to think that they have been hurt by my kindness." He closes his eyes, almost like he's fighting tears, but then he looks back at the camera with a soft smile. "I appreciate your time in listening to this message. Thank you for being willing to hear the truth."

Then the video ends.

Dad and I are silent, processing what just happened.

"Well, there's a reason why he's a good actor," Dad finally says.

"You've got to be flipping kidding me," I mutter. "This is ridiculous! He's lying!"

"Oh, I know. But it's so easy for men to manipulate the public perception, even when you have multiple women coming forward."

"But there's seven women in the article!" I exclaim.

My dad just scrolls down the comments and shows me the dozens that are already rolling in.

I knew you were innocent, Tristan!

The truth always comes out.

Even if he was a womanizer, I'd still want him.

There are a lot more crude comments, mostly derogatory names for the women cited in the original article.

Anger rolls through my body, pulsing in my veins. "This is an outrage." I look up at my dad. "You know this industry. What can we do now?"

He heaves a sigh. "There isn't much we *can* do at this point. Adam's name hasn't been brought up in this controversy, but it hasn't made Tristan look like the villain you thought it would. Despite all of this, I'm pretty sure the production company will still want Tristan instead of Adam."

He looks down at his phone and grimaces. "Ugh. The weird commenters are back again."

"Who?" I peer over his shoulder at the screen and read the comments he's referring to.

Lionel: This is false!

Brigette: Tristan is a liar! We want Adam Stone back on screen!

Josephine: Don't believe this!

I stifle a laugh, hiding my face behind my hand.

"Do you know who these people are? They were all over the first article, too."

I nod. "It's the staff at Stone Castle. I guess they're joining the fight in their own little way."

The side of my dad's mouth lifts in a half-smile. "I should've known. I remember Lionel and Brigette. She seemed...very sweet."

I nod in agreement. But the smile on my face slowly fades as I think about how Adam must be feeling right now. Does he even know what's going on? I don't know if he wants to follow everything online after I left. Whether or not he is, I want to be with him. The pull is so strong and so urgent, I grab my bag off the table and announce to my dad, "I have to go."

"Go? Now?"

I nod. "I need to be with Adam. If this is the end of his career, I want to be with him so he's not alone."

My dad sighs. "As your manager, I have to highly discourage this. You need to have a public appearance and show that you're not fazed by anything going on."

My hands clench into fists. "I'm not doing the movie with Tristan. I *am* fazed by what's going on. I won't just pretend everything is okay."

"You didn't let me finish." He pauses. "As your manager, I would advise you to go forward and do the movie. But as your father...I want you to go to Adam."

I rush him with a hug and bend down to kiss him on the cheek. "Thank you, Dad. I'll be in touch."

"Drive safely."

I nod and rush out the door to the one person I need right now.

Adam.

Thirty-Five

ADAM

The rain continues to pour. Maybe Lionel is right about the myth, after all. Because my mood has never been stormier.

I'm almost tempted to break into the liquor cabinet. But I still won't do that. Not after the promise I made to Lily. I can imagine her waggling a finger at my face. *No sad drinking, Adam.*

I close my eyes, resting my head on the wingback chair of the study. The fire roars in front of me. With my eyes closed, I can picture the night I found Isabelle in the forest, sitting here with her in my arms. The first night I truly let my guard down with her and knew there was something exceptionally incredible about the woman I held.

It almost feels like a dream now. She's gone, and everything is back to the way it was. I'm alone, and I've ruined my career. Isabelle hasn't contacted me in the last week, and how could she? We didn't even exchange phone numbers. I could ask Jim, but that would seem desperate. I've stayed away from any news sites, knowing that any reports about her and Tristan would just drive me mad.

I figure she's realized how ridiculous our little tryst was. It was a matter of convenience. She was stuck here, I'm a man, she's a woman—isn't that how all the storybooks go? They fall in love because there's nothing else to do.

To me, it was real. If I'd met Isabelle any other time or place, I'd know that she was the one I was meant to be with. But I would never subject her to be stuck with a beast of a man like me.

A loud knock sounds on the front door. I listen for Lionel to go open it, wondering who would be here at this time of night, and in this rain. The snow has mostly melted, but there are patches of slush all around the castle. All the beauty from the snow is gone, replaced with dirty brown splotches and a gray sky.

I wait a minute but don't hear anything from Lionel. The knock sounds again.

"Fine, fine, I'll get it," I mutter to no one, getting out of my chair. I trudge to the front entryway, pull the door open, and see...

Isabelle.

My Belle.

Soaking wet, with rain dropping on her head, and a huge smile lighting her face.

Before I can tell her to come inside and get warm, she yanks my shirt, pulling me outside in the rain with her, and kissing me square on the lips.

I'm still in shock, and it takes a minute to process what's happening. Isabelle is HERE, not THERE, and she's in my arms and her lips are on mine...and now that my mind has caught up to the present, I hold on to her tightly, never wanting to let her go.

I can't believe I let her leave in the first place.

Her foot slips in the rain, and we both go down. We both land on our backs, but I keep one arm under her upper body to break her fall. Propped up on one arm, the other hand on my chest, she leans down to kiss me again, and I feel like I'm whole.

"You came back," I whisper.

She nods. "I'm sorry I left at all." She gently runs her hand down my face. "I'm just glad I'm here with you now."

"Why? Do you think I'm dying?" I ask with a laugh.

She smiles. "No, I didn't think that. But I shouldn't have left you all alone to deal with the fallout. We should have been together. At least now we can be."

I reach my hand up to her face and stroke her cheek. Her skin is so soft, and I've missed her terribly. So, I tell her. "I missed you so much."

She blinks, and I think she's holding back tears. "I missed you, too." She leans down and kisses me one more time. "I love you, Adam."

The weight of her words hits my chest, and it's like my life is complete now. "I love you, too, Belle."

She laughs and rests her head on my chest, and suddenly, the rain clears. The sun peeks out from behind the clouds. Isabelle sits up and looks at the blue expanse stretching over us, dotted with clouds. It's like the heavens themselves have opened and shine down on us, warming my skin and lighting my beautiful Belle. "Well, that was interesting timing."

I look up at her, illuminated by the picturesque sky and sun behind her, and think how much she's been an angel to me, sent to heal me and my life. She appeared when I least deserved her and healed every piece of me that seemed unreachable. She is everything I need and more than I could hope for. In this moment, I realize something else.

"Isabelle," I whisper. "My sight. It's back."

"What?"

"I thought it's been returning. I've had little flashes here and there, but I wasn't sure. But now...I think it's back for good."

Her eyes widen. "Really?"

"Really. Test it out."

She covers my good eye with one hand and holds up the other. "How many fingers am I holding up?"

"Five."

"And now?"

"Three."

"What color are my eyes?"

I pull her hand off my face. "Brown. But I would know that with both eyes covered."

She laughs and holds me again, leaning her head on my chest. "I can't believe it."

I wrap my arms around her, contentment running through my body. "Even if I were blind in both eyes, I would be happy to just be here with you."

Before she can respond, Lionel's voice sounds from inside the castle. "Mr. Stone? And...Ms. Lovett? Is that you?"

"Yes, it's me!" Isabelle says cheerily. "It's good to see you, Lionel. And thank you and the rest of the staff for your attempts to help."

"Help?" I ask, turning to Isabelle. "What does that mean?"

She waves a hand. "We'll talk about it later."

Lionel has a faint blush but just clears his throat. "Mr. Stone, your sister is calling."

Reluctantly, Isabelle and I stand and walk to Lionel.

"Perhaps you'd like to dry off first?" he asks.

"Yes." I look over at Isabelle. "I'll meet you in the theater? We'll talk to Lily there."

She nods and kisses me once more.

I tell Lionel to relay the message to Lily, take the fastest shower of my life, and head into the theater. I'm unsure what

Lily wants, but I'm also anxious to be with Isabelle. To my surprise, Isabelle walks in a minute later. She settles in next to me on the couch, and I take a moment to relish the fact that she's here next to me.

Isabelle leans her head on my shoulder and sighs. "All right. Let's call Lily."

I pull out my phone and dial her number, and Lily answers right away.

"Hey, Adam," Lily says.

"Hey, Lily. I'm here with Isabelle. Everything okay?"

"Oh! Hey, Isabelle. Um, yes. Well, you might not agree, because you're so worried about protecting me and all that, but everything is fine. I'm fine. You're fine. Or, you're going to be."

"Lily. Stop rambling. What's going on?"

Isabelle speaks up. "Is this about the articles?"

I turn to her. "What articles?"

Isabelle's mouth opens, then closes. "You don't know anything?"

I shake my head slightly, and Lily speaks. "I'm going to send you a couple of links. Don't overreact."

Those are two words I really don't like. "What is happening?"

"Bye, Adam!"

She hangs up. I look over at Isabelle. "Do you know what that's all about?"

Isabelle bites her lip. "I might have an idea."

The phone buzzes in my hand. First is a link to an article. I click it and read yet another article by my dear friend Allegra at Inside Scoop. The article talks about five women who claim that Tristan Jackson manipulated them into falling in love with them, only for him to take something from them (money, an opportunity, a connection) and leave them heartbroken and alone.

Sounds familiar.

"Did you have something to do with this?" I ask Isabelle.

She nods reluctantly. "I was trying to build a case against Tristan."

"And?"

She shakes her head slightly. "I'm so sorry, Adam. It didn't work. It's not getting the negative reaction I thought it would, and then Tristan published his own video, feigning ignorance and fake-apologizing for these women misinterpreting his intentions." She squeezes my arm. "But I've already talked to my dad. I won't do the movie with him. I don't care what this does to my acting career. The truth—and you—matter more than getting ahead as an actress."

I shake my head in disbelief. "I can't believe you went through all of that for me."

"It was for you, but it was also for those women. And to get some kind of justice against Tristan. I'm embarrassed that I thought it would work."

I kiss the top of her head. "Just trying means more to me than you'll know. And we'll get you into acting, I know it."

My phone buzzes in my hand again with a new text from Lily. It's a YouTube video link. I click it, and upon reading the title, I start to panic.

TRISTAN JACKSON EXPOSED FOR MANIPULATING A MINOR

Instead of a reporter, I see my little sister's sweet face fill the screen. Isabelle gasps beside me. "I didn't think she was going to say anything..."

"She can't!" I exclaim. "The contract."

Isabelle shakes her head. "Lily told me she never signed it. It's invalid, at least on her end."

I don't even have a minute to process her words before Lily speaks on the screen.

"Hi, everyone. My name is Lily Stone, and I'm going to tell you the story of how Tristan Jackson ruined my life."

I can't tear my eyes from the screen as I watch my sister detail parts of the story I haven't even heard. How Tristan met her at a party in Hollywood that she had attended with me when she was only seventeen. How he got her number and started texting her innocuously, then slowly started feeding her lines about how she was so special and different from all the other girls. That age meant nothing, and she was wise beyond her years. How he promised that she was the only one he'd ever love. With each claim, images from her phone appear on the screen, proof of these messages that he sent her.

My stomach tightens as I hear her give all these details that she never expressly told me. I didn't want to know everything. Hearing it directly from her mouth, anger in her expression and voice, also fills me with pride that she's now strong enough to express herself.

Her eyes shine with tears as she continues. "I was so dumb to believe him, but can you blame me? All I wanted was to be seen and feel special, like I mattered to someone. And Tristan filled that need, but not because he truly felt that way about me. It was because he knew that I was naive and weak and easily manipulated."

She takes in a shaky breath and continues. "Anyway, right after I turned eighteen, Tristan told me he wanted to get married." She leans toward the camera. "Yes. Married. And his plan was to take me away the night of the Goldies. I was at a different event with my other brother, Henry, when I got a frantic text from Tristan saying that Adam had punched him on the red carpet and we needed to leave earlier than expected. So I rushed out of the event and met up with him." She pulls her long hair over her shoulder and fiddles with it. "We got to Vegas, and I thought we were going to get married right away, but he kept delaying for a few days, saying he wanted every-thing to be 'perfect.' What I didn't know was that he was waiting for Adam to show up. And he did."

She tosses her hair over her shoulder and continues. "Adam came for me, along with our brother Henry." She shakes her head and laughs. "It was as if we were in a movie. Adam storms in, accusing Tristan of taking advantage of me to get back at him. The whole time, I'm crying and swearing that Tristan loves me, that he's wrong, until my brothers proved he was right. By offering him a check in exchange for me."

Her eyes flick upward, and I can tell she's holding back tears. Isabelle's hold on my arm tightens. I just want to reach through the screen and hold Lily close, telling her that she doesn't need to do this. She doesn't need to tell her story. She can stay safe where she is, and we'll protect her forever.

But she looks back at the camera and speaks again. "I've never been so humiliated in my life. Tristan found the right person who would fall for his wiles, and preyed on my inno-cence and naivete. For what?" She leans in. "All Tristan wanted to do was get back at my brother for some past disagreement between them. I don't even know what happened. For years, he's been fooling everyone in the industry into thinking he's Hollywood's 'golden boy,' and that he can do no wrong. But I'm here to tell you that he can. And anyone who thinks Adam Stone is the problem needs to hear this side of the story. Adam signed an agreement to never speak about this because he wanted to keep me safe. But I never signed anything. And if telling the truth is going to clear Adam's name, then I'm happy to do something for my big brother, who loves me more than anything in the world." She hesitates with a smile. "Well, maybe not anymore."

I chuckle, knowing she's referring to Isabelle.

"I hope you'll respect my right to privacy," Lily continues on camera. "But I know that's not realistic to expect. I will not be responding to any requests for more information or interviews. Thank you for listening, and please share this video."

The video ends.

"I can't believe she did that," Isabelle murmurs beside me.

I stare at the screen. "Me neither. But...I'm proud of her."

Isabelle nods in agreement. "What are the comments saying?"

I click on the screen. "Lily turned comments off, which is probably a smart move." I call Lily right away, and she answers.

"You watched it." She's not asking; she knows.

"I did."

"Are you angry with me?"

Am I? I've been saying for months that she needs to be kept in our family's apartment to stay safe. That we needed to shield her from the world and anyone or anything that could hurt her. That she couldn't handle being on her own yet.

But now she proved that she can handle herself, that she's brave and strong and willing to sacrifice herself to protect me.

The way I've done for her.

"No," I finally say. "I'm not angry. I'm proud of you."

Her voice is quiet. "Thank you."

"But I'm also worried for you," I add. "I don't know if you understand what this will mean."

"I have an idea. Don't worry, I'm not watching the video to see how many views it has. And I won't check articles about it. I'm sure people won't believe my story, but we know it's true. And maybe with my first-hand account, it'll make enough of a difference to the movie production company to change their mind."

"And Tristan—"

"We'll deal with Tristan if we need to," Lily says. "But it was my turn to protect you."

My throat constricts, tight with a sudden wave of emotion. "Either way, thank you for trying to clear my name."

"Anything for you," she says. "You saved me. I love you."

I swallow hard. "I love you, too. You, uh, stay safe, okay? We'll talk later."

"Sounds good."

We hang up, and I sit back on the couch in a daze. My sister came forward. The truth is out there.

"Now what?" I ask out loud.

"We wait," Isabelle replies. "Together."

I look over at the perfect woman in my arm, filled with gratitude that she's seen me this whole time. Even if no one else changes their opinion of me, at least I have her. And that's all that matters.

"And in the meantime," she adds, "let's watch a movie."

Epilogue
ISABELLE

THREE MONTHS LATER (AUGUST)

"Action!" calls the director. I'm standing on the side of the stage, watching the scene begin in front of me. Since I enter halfway through, I run my first line through my mind to embody my character: Holly, who was living in the big city for ten years before returning to her hometown and falling back in love with the man who stole her heart as a teenager. Cliché? Abso-flipping-lutely. Yet, it's been my favorite role to act. Who knew I'd be such a sucker for these cheesy love stories?

The man from Holly's hometown, Chase, is on the phone in his hardware shop, clearly distressed because he thinks Holly moved back home to the big city and his sister will never get the medical treatment she needs if he doesn't get married by tomorrow. Don't ask about the details. They're not important.

"She's gone, Mags," he says. "I don't think she's coming back. I'm so sorry. I—" He clears his throat, overcome with emotion. "I wish there was more we could do for you. Thanks. Love you, too."

The actor for Chase hangs up the phone, rubs his forehead with his hand, and that's my cue to enter. I step through the set door to his shop, dressed in fitted jeans and cowgirl boots, my hands in my pockets. The bell above the door jingles, and Chase looks up.

His eyes are overcome with emotion, and I feel like he really believes this moment like I do. "Holly," he whispers. "What are you doing here?"

"I'm back," I say, a small smile on my face. "I tried to leave, but my heart pulled me back. I can't be anywhere other than here in Apple Town."

"Oh. So...it's the town." He swallows. "I'm sure Beckanne will be glad to see that you're back." He turns around, busying himself with something on the cash register.

I step closer to him until the counter is the only thing between us. "I hope so, but I'm not here for her."

"Hmm?" he asks, not turning to see me.

"I'm here for *you*, Chase."

Those words make him turn and look me in the eye.

"I love you," I say, my throat catching with emotion. "I always have. I lost myself for a time, but you've shown me who I really am and that I belong here. With you."

"You really mean it?" he asks. "You better not be yanking my chain, because I don't think I can—"

He doesn't finish that sentence, because I grab his shirt from across the counter and pull him toward me, kissing him. Our lips are locked for a few seconds before I pull back and say, "I really mean it."

"Good," he replies. "Because I love you, too."

We kiss again until the director calls, "Cut! Great job, you two! That was the best yet. We'll take a break."

I look back at my costar—the love of my life, Adam Stone—and ask, "Now why do you think that was the best yet?"

He smirks at me. "Probably because we've kissed a million times by now."

I press a quick kiss to his lips. "A million and one."

He comes around the counter and slips an arm around my waist. "Do you want a snack? Or a drink?"

"Let's grab some food," I reply. We head over to the craft services table and serve up a couple of plates. The production team was shocked at first when Adam was serving himself instead of demanding people get everything for him, but now they're used to it. I think they were all afraid of him, but they've been pleasantly surprised by his change of heart. Every now and then, I have to remind him to take a deep breath to calm his frustration, but overall, he's done the work himself.

"We need to go see Lily this weekend," Adam says quietly. "Henry and Luna will be there, too."

I nod in agreement. "Is he officially–"

Adam hums and nods, but we can't say more here. Her video had a greater effect than we could have even anticipated. The entire public opinion of Tristan Jackson shifted, especially considering the proof she provided in her video. He's disappeared completely, and there's no word of him getting a role again in the future. That was good news at first, but there were rumors of Tristan taking legal action against her for defamation of character. So instead of letting her out of isolation, like they had anticipated doing by now, her family doubled down on her lockdown.

"I've been talking to Aunt Agatha, and we might have a solution."

"Oh?"

He nods. "We'll talk to Lily about it this weekend. How would you feel about taking a trip to the castle, as well?"

"My dad's been wanting to see Brigette. Maybe we'll all go together."

Yes, that's right. My dad and Brigette are *dating*. I'd be weirded out if I didn't love Brigette so much. Dad has also lightened his workload, focusing only on managing me and Adam now. We still have moments of conflict as he navigates our dual-sided relationship, but we're finding a better balance. I think he's realizing how much his work took away from family life, and he wants to be part of the important things now.

"All right, let's go again!" the director calls.

I look up at him. "You ready?"

"Ready."

Together, instead of just watching a movie, we make one.

WE'RE DRIVING up the winding road to the castle again, but this time I actually get to enjoy the view. It turns out the drive is quite beautiful when I'm not the one driving the car. And when it's not, you know, SNOWING. Since it's August, it's pretty warm at three in the afternoon, but it's a dry heat so it's fairly comfortable.

Adam laces his fingers through mine, and I smile at him. He gives me the half-grin I love so much, and my heart still flutters in my chest.

"How much longer is it?" Dad asks from the back seat.

Oh, yeah. Dad is with us, too.

"Just another mile and a half," Adam replies. "We're nearly there."

Dad sits back in his seat and sighs. I guess he's pretty anxious to see Brigette again. It's weird to watch your dad date, but I'm genuinely happy for him. Especially after his whole speech to me about how love can be hard, it makes me feel good to know that he's found someone that might make the hard times worth it.

Just like Adam is for me.

"I wanted to talk to you, Adam," Dad says. "I'm getting constant phone calls now asking for interviews with Lily. It seems like she's dropped off the face of the planet, but people want to hear more from her."

"No." Adam's response is immediate.

"Even just a quick–"

"Absolutely not."

Dad huffs and sits back in his seat. I have to admit, it's nice that Dad and Adam already had a relationship with each other. I can only imagine bringing Adam home to meet my dad for the first time if they hadn't known each other before. *Hey, Dad, this is Adam Stone. He's a little blunt and gruff, but don't take it personally.* I don't think that would've gone over so well. Instead, they've already known each other for years, so there's no need to sugarcoat Adam's personality. Adam's not really on his best behavior for Dad, and Dad isn't put off when Adam acts like... well, himself.

Overall, Adam has gotten a lot better. He's kind and considerate, especially toward me, but even toward the people he works with and those who work for him. But when it comes to Lily, he doesn't beat around the bush. He wants to protect his sister with his last breath.

A few minutes later, we pull up to the castle. It looks so different from when I arrived three months ago, but it's still so beautiful. I exhale, and smile at Adam. In a weird way, it's like coming home.

Just as expected, Lionel stands outside to greet us. Adam drives around the driveway and puts the car in park, and Lionel opens my door. "Ms. Isabelle, it's wonderful to see you again."

"You, too, Lionel," I say, squeezing him in a hug. It's not the most comfortable hug I've ever had, but it makes my heart happy. "How's Josephine?"

"She's…well." The faint blush on his cheeks lets me know things are going well between them, but I won't press any more. "Hello, Mr. Lovett," he says to my dad.

Dad shakes his hand, and Adam comes around the car to shake Lionel's hand, as well. "Are we all set?" Adam asks.

Lionel nods. "Everything is nearly in order."

"Good." Adam presses a hand to the small of my back, leading me into the castle. Dad follows behind.

"What does he mean that everything is nearly in order?" I ask Adam.

Adam waves me off. "I have to get something from the office. Join me?"

I raise a brow at him. "I'm allowed in there now?"

He presses a kiss to my temple. "You're allowed in every part of my life now."

My heart warms. We go up the stairs, and Dad waves goodbye as he heads down the corridor to find Brigette.

"What's in the office that you need?" I ask.

"Something for Lily," he replies. We step into the office, and he heads over to the desk, then pulls the old photo of his family into his hands. His fingers lightly trace the crack on the glass, the one I made the first night I came here, and a sad smile appears on his face.

"I want Lily to have this," he says. "It was a reminder of my mother and the way she raised us to be. To take care of each other, no matter what. I want Lily to have it so she knows I'm doing this all for her."

I press a kiss to his cheek. "I know you're doing your best to protect her."

He straightens. "Enough of this. Would you like to go watch a movie while we wait for dinner?"

"Really? That's what you want to do while we're here?"

He pulls me in by the waist, pressing my body flush against his. "Well, there might be some of this, too." He kisses me, and my body hums as I feel the passion flowing from him.

I love this man.

We head to the theater, and Adam grabs The Sound of Music from the shelf. "Don't worry, we'll stop the movie once Georg and Maria get together," he says.

"Good," I reply. "I know it's a happy ending, but—"

"But you hate that they have to leave. I know." He has a twinkle in his eye as he settles in beside me and we start watching the rolling hills of Austria.

WE HAVE Lionel bring us dinner in the theater so we can enjoy the movie and give Dad some private time with Brigette. As soon as the scene in the gazebo is over, where Georg and Maria sing about their love for each other, Adam and I turn off the movie and leave the theater.

"Where to?" I ask.

"I have something to show you outside," he says. Taking me by the hand, he leads me out the front doors of the castle and over to the right. The sun has just set, stars beginning to twinkle in the sky, and the moon casts a glow over us. We pass a row of roses, red and pink and purple and yellow, glinting in the night.

Adam stops, still holding my hand. "This was my mother's garden," he says. "It hasn't bloomed yet since her death."

We stand still for a few minutes, breathing in the fragrance and soaking in the colors. "It's beautiful," I say. "Thank you for showing me."

"This isn't why I brought you out here though," he says.

"No?"

He starts walking again, and we follow the glowing light of the moon to a gazebo in the middle of the field.

"Where did this come from?" I ask. "I don't remember it when we were here in May."

"It's a new addition," he replies. "Want to check it out?"

My heart starts hammering in my chest. Could this...is he...

We step inside the gazebo, and I take in my surroundings in wonder. It's a perfect replica of the gazebo in The Sound of Music: white painted wood for the structure, glass panes that allow the moonlight to stream in, and white stone benches in a circle. There are lit candles on all the benches and around the floor.

Our hands still entwined, Adam draws me in close to him. "I remember the first night you came to the castle," he says. "You threw me off balance."

"Oh, did I?" I ask.

He smirks. "I was so flustered. That's why I made you wait two hours for dinner."

I chuckle. "Now I get it."

"And then at dinner, I was determined to show you exactly who I was, so you wouldn't have any misconceptions about working with me." He shakes his head. "But instead of cowering, you met me as an equal. And you set me in my place."

"And I missed my chance for a dramatic exit with that snowstorm."

"True, but I'll be forever grateful for the snowstorm that forced you to stay." He holds me close, leaning his forehead down on mine.

"I'm grateful, too," I say softly.

"You broke me down, bit by bit, and then rebuilt the pieces. I don't know what I've ever done to deserve you, but I'm never letting you go."

"You must have done something good," I say with a smile, referencing the song we just watched from The Sound of Music.

He smiles. "Maybe. No matter what the reason, I want you to be mine. Forever." He lowers himself to one knee, and out of his pocket, he pulls out a ring. It looks antique, with delicate engravings on the gold that wraps around the gems. The center is a round diamond, surrounded by tiny rubies. "Belle, I never want you to leave my side. You make me a better man than I ever thought possible. Will you marry me?"

Tears fill my eyes, but the answer is immediate. "Yes, yes!"

He stands and slips the ring on my finger, wrapping his arms around my waist and pulling me in for a kiss. This moment feels almost like a movie, with the glittering lights of the candles and the stars above us. But there's even more— there's depth and history and love, a shared connection I feel from my lips down to my toes. Adam is part of me now, and no matter how hard things may get in our real life, this love that we have is worth every moment.

So I have to admit, real life is even better than the movies.

THE END

Keep reading for a sneak peek at Lily's story, Lily of the Tower!

<h1 style="text-align:center">*Bonus Epilogue*</h1>

LILY

My fingers fly over the keys, playing Chopin's Fantasie-Impromptu. It's considered one of the most difficult pieces to master on the piano, and I've got it down. That's what eleven months in isolation will do for a pianist.

The elevator doors open to my side, but I don't bother looking over. I know who it is. Henry, Luna, Adam, and Isabelle said they wanted to visit today. They're the only visitors I've had, so it's no surprise. Father is reading a book on the couch while I play the piano, and he stands to greet them, giving me the time I need to finish playing my piece.

I hear their murmured voices behind me, but I concentrate on the music. There's nothing worse than playing perfectly, only to mess up the last few bars before the end. My day could be ruined until I attempt it again.

Thankfully, I finish it in peace, only making a few slip-ups that I notice, but nothing audible to my audience. They clap for me, and I stand from the bench. "Thank you, thank you," I say, taking a mock bow. My long, blonde braid falls to the side. It's longer than ever, since I haven't left home to get a haircut in almost a year. I can actually sit on my hair now.

The light streams through the floor-to-ceiling windows, the perfect golden-hour sun illuminating our home. We've lived in this penthouse since I was born, and it's the only home I've known. Unfortunately, I've gotten to know it way too well over the last year. The polished concrete and natural wood interior used to feel like home, but now it feels like a prison. Sometimes I get to spend a few hours on the wraparound balcony and soak in the sun, smelling the flowers that my mother loved to decorate along the edges, but most of my time is spent inside these days. And, of course, all the state-of-the-art technology to ensure that no one will enter...and that I don't leave.

"Maybe I can perform for a *real* audience one of these days," I say to the small group, raising a brow.

My brothers exchange a glance.

"Well, that's not encouraging," I say.

"Sit, Lily," Henry says, gesturing at the couch.

I watch them warily as I lower myself to sitting. Father sits in the wingback chair next to the couch, and my brothers sit on either side of me, their fiancées on their other sides.

Fiancées. The word reminds me that I haven't seen Isabelle's ring yet. I reach around Adam and grab Isabelle's hand, admiring the antique setting and perfect stones he chose for her. "It's gorgeous," I say.

She grins at me, then glances at Adam. "Thanks, Lily. He did a good job picking it out."

These girls have no idea how much I've helped my brothers pick out their rings. The boys video chatted with me from the jewelry stores, asking my opinion and *thankfully* listening when I told them not to go with a traditional princess cut diamond. But I like to let my brothers have the credit. After all, they're the ones who are smart enough to ask for my opinion.

Henry and Luna were supposed to get married this summer. But Luna, the sweetheart she is, wanted to postpone the wedding. It won't be a tiny, private affair, since *everyone* loves the two of them, so they wanted to wait for me so I could be there.

Maybe that's why they're here.

"Have you set a date?" I ask them. "Is the wedding happening soon?"

Henry and Luna exchange a glance. "Uh, not quite," Henry replies.

"Oh." I slump down in my seat. "Well, spit it out, then. Don't leave me hanging."

Adam's phone starts ringing. "Finally," he mutters and answers it. On the screen, I see our brother, Peter, in some tropical location with a drink in his hand.

"Hey, everyone!" he calls, his voice loud and cheerful. "Lily, is that you?"

"Peter!" I grab the phone from Adam. "Where are you?"

"I'm in the Maldives! It's so fantastic. You'll have to come visit!"

Adam snatches the phone from me. "Peter, we've already discussed this."

"Oh, right." Peter sets down his drink and fixes the camera with a mock glare. "This is a very serious conversation," he says, lowering his voice.

"Is it?" I ask. "No one will tell me anything."

Adam sets the phone down on the coffee table so we can all see Peter, the side of his mouth turned up in a grin. I don't think I've *ever* seen him take anything seriously. The sounds of people partying at the pool behind him are an interesting backdrop to what's supposed to be a serious conversation.

Henry clears his throat to begin. "As you know, the video you posted created...quite a stir."

"Isabelle's father says he's fielding requests for interviews from you left and right," Adam adds.

I shrug. "Okay, so? That's nothing new. Just keep telling them no. I don't want to talk about it anymore."

"Yes, he's been doing that," Adam says. "But we're getting to a point where we're concerned."

I furrow my brow. "Concerned? About what? I've been up here for almost a year now. I think it's about time you let me out again."

Henry clears his throat. "There have been rumors that Tristan is upset about the video."

I snort. "As he should be."

"He's suing you," Adam finally says. "For defamation of character."

I bite my lip, managing a little, "Oh."

It's totally unexpected, but hearing that he's finally taking some kind of action makes my heart rate pick up a little bit. I know in my head that I shouldn't care about him. But when there's someone out there who wishes you harm, it's a little hard to swallow, especially for a people-pleaser like me.

"We want to move you," Father says gently. "To live with Agatha in Brookhaven."

It takes a couple of beats for that to sink in. They want to move me from here to live with crazy Aunt Agatha? Well, she is crazy, but I do adore her. It might not be terrible.

"I guess that's okay," I reply slowly. "For how long?"

My brothers and dad exchange a glance. "We're not sure," Henry replies. "We want to keep you safe a little longer, at the very least until the lawyers can get a look at everything and see what they can do for the case."

A tiny spark of hope flares in me. "But I can go out, right? Brookhaven is tiny. There's no way anything bad would happen to me there. It's not a big city like here in Silver Lake."

Henry doesn't look at me. Father presses his lips together.

"Not yet," Adam says. "We don't know what kind of tactics Tristan could use."

"Come *on*," I plead. "He's not like that."

"Oh?" Adam says. "What is he like? Tell me, Lily. Did you think he was the type of person who could convince you to run off to Vegas, only to—"

Isabelle places a gentle hand on his arm, and Adam stops talking. He takes in a cleansing breath and exhales.

"Wow. Impressive," I say to Isabelle.

She smiles softly at me.

Adam reaches into her bag, pulling out a picture frame. "I want you to have this."

I take the frame from him, a picture of our family when we were whole. Father, Mom, my three brothers, and me. It's about fifteen years old, so I was only four there, but I can still feel the love like it was yesterday. My mother's death wrecked us all... possibly me the most.

But the frame has a crack in it. I touch it lightly with my fingers. "Why is it broken?"

"That's my fault," Isabelle says. "I knocked it down while I was at the castle."

"It was quite a first impression," Adam says, giving her a tender glance I don't think I *ever* expected to come from him. "But it brought that picture to the forefront, and it helped guide me back to where I am now." He touches my shoulder lightly. "I think Mom would have wanted you to be safe, Lily. And Aunt Agatha is happy to take you in. Besides, you could really use a change of scenery, right?"

I sniff and blink away my tears. While I'm not sure that Mom would have been completely on board with the way I've been locked up for the last year, I want our family to be whole again. I want to be back to the way we were in the picture.

The tender moment is broken by a loud voice from Adam's phone. "Heyyyyy, Peter!"

We all turn our heads and see Peter giving a bro-hand-shake/hug to another man.

"Ryder!" Peter points at the phone. "Hey, I'm on a call right now but let's get some drinks later!"

Ryder looks into the camera, and I have to suck in a breath. Dark hair swooping over his forehead, gray eyes, and a smile that could melt an iceberg.

No, Lily. Don't get sucked in by attractive looks and a charismatic smile. That was exactly where you went wrong with Tristan.

"Is that your family?" Ryder asks. He waves at the camera. "Hey, everyone!"

"Do you guys remember Ryder?" Peter asks. "He's Wendi–I mean Gwen Darling's cousin."

"Peter, this is not the time," Adam growls.

"Right, right." Peter mumbles something to Ryder, who walks out of view of the camera. But we still hear him say, "Your sister is cute."

My cheeks flame with heat. Adam's hands clench into fists, and Henry sits forward in his seat. On screen, Peter looks over at Ryder and scowls. "Don't even think about it."

Okay, there's that. I guess I should've expected my brothers to panic at the sign of a man having any kind of reaction to me. I exhale, a little shaken at semi-interacting with an attractive man for the first time in nearly a year, and I'm admittedly flattered. No wonder I'm a mess. If I'm not careful, I'm going to fall for the first man with a charming grin.

"Okay, so Brookhaven," I say, eager to turn the conversation back to where we left off. "You want me to live with Agatha."

"Yes," Father replies. "You know she has that tower in her home."

"That's right. What's the tower for exactly?" I ask.

The men all shake their heads. "We don't question Agatha," Henry finally says.

"Does she have a piano?" I ask. "That's non-negotiable."

"Yes," Adam says quickly. "She reassured me that she does."

"Okay." I sit and think, but really, what choice do I have? I've proven myself unworthy of making my own decisions. No one trusts my judgment anymore. I'm not sure what option I have other than to go along with the plan.

"Fine, I'll go," I say.

Everyone smiles, and Henry wraps me in a hug. "I promise it's for your benefit."

I nod into his shoulder and pray that he's right.

Besides, it's only temporary.

Thank you for reading Isabelle and the Beast! I hope you truly enjoyed my version of the classic fairy tale, Beauty and the Beast.

I know that a big part of why people, especially readers, love this fairy tale is because the Disney version features Belle as a reader, and one of the best parts of the cartoon is the Beast's library. But I wanted to find my own version of the original fairy tale instead of sticking to the Disney version (for multiple reasons), and I hope you enjoyed Adam and Isabelle sharing their special times in the theater, bonding over their love of movies.

If you enjoyed this story, I'd love for you to leave a review! Lily of the Tower will be next, and I hope you will read that one, as well!

Acknowledgments

First of all, I want to thank my readers. You were been so patient with me while I wrote and prepared this story, but you never wavered in your enthusiasm for Adam and Isabelle. I'm so grateful for the amount of love shown for both Cinder Luna as well as me. You readers are what make this all worth it, and I'm so grateful there are people who actually enjoy what I write.

My beta readers, you ladies are the MVPs. Lola (I think you read it three times!), Christina, and Haley—you're so incredibly helpful and always pull the best stories out of me. Thank you for taking the time to read my stories and for always being so thoughtful in your suggestions.

Melody, you killed it again with this cover. I love our relationship, and I'm so thankful that your work inspires me to write!

Jennifer, you're the best editor. I honestly don't see myself publishing without your eyes on my words!

Sarah, I've been so grateful for your help, especially this year. Thank you for keeping everything running smoothly while I took care of the baby! And thank you for always being there to bounce ideas off of.

My author friends—Monique, Anne, Sara, Elysia, Patty, and so many others—you've been the best supporters. Even the way we just cheer each other on while writing has been a huge motivation.

My husband, Caleb. You're literally sitting on the floor with the baby as I write this, and I'm so thankful you've supported me for the last three years as I've followed my dream to become an author. Not only do you encourage me to pursue my passions, you're the inspiration for all the love stories I write. Our story is my favorite. Love is hard, but you make it so worthwhile, each and every day.

My kiddos, thank you for being so enthusiastic and sweet about Mommy's writing. I hope you realize that you can follow your dreams, too.

And finally, I am so thankful to my God for every blessing I have—my husband, my family, and the life we enjoy—and I thank Him for the ability to write stories and share them with others.

Also by Marie Soleil

Canyon Cove Love Stories

Speak Your Truth

Feel the Rhythm

Let Love In

Take a Chance

Standalone Stories

Exceptional Emma

Love is a Roller Coaster

Once Upon a Rom-Com

Cookies & Kisses

Cinder Luna

Isabelle and the Beast

Lily of the Tower

Wendi & Peter

About the Author

Marie has had two goals since she was seven years old: to be a mother, and to be an author. She has been a storyteller her whole life and loves sharing these stories with the world. When she's not writing, she can be found watching The Office, playing the piano, sewing a dress, or reading a book (while consuming copious amounts of chocolate). She lives in sunny Southern California with her husband of 16 years, four children, and their chickens.